Skin Deep

Vera Berry Burrows

A Wings ePress, Inc.
Mainstream Fiction Novel

Wings ePress, Inc.

Edited by: Jeanne Smith
Copy Edited by: Christie Kraemer
Executive Editor: Jeanne Smith
Cover Artist: Trisha FitzGerald-Jung

All rights reserved

Wings ePress Books
www.wingsepress.com

Copyright © 2020 by: Vera Berry Burrows
ISBN 978-1-61309-567-6

Published In the United States Of America

Wings ePress Inc.
3000 N. Rock Road
Newton, KS 67114

What They Are Saying About
Skin Deep

Skin Deep is a romance that portrays the challenges many Jamaican immigrants to the UK faced in the period shortly after the end of the Second World War. BJ and Emma are the main characters, forced to keep their love secret due to the prejudices of the day, which were widespread against people of different ethnic backgrounds. They are separated by the challenges they face and this book makes the reader want to discover if they can overcome and find true love. This is a story which was a sad truth for many couples of this era. A thoroughly enjoyable read.

—Janet Muskett, Helensvale, Gold Coast, Queensland

Skin Deep is a powerful reflection of post-World War Two Britain in which two young lovers are forced to confront simmering racial discrimination. Emma and BJ know that their unstoppable, passionate affair is pitted against all odds and which ultimately is to crash and burn, leaving an innocent young mixed-race child searching for identity and acceptance. It is pure fiction but could so easily be fact. Vera Berry Burrows has skilfully woven romance, intrigue and suspense into a story of humanity's darkest failure that is as much alive and relevant today as it was generations ago. It's a great read and a story that I, for one, hope will have a sequel.

—Ernest Allenbrook, former UK newspaper journalist and author.

Another excellent novel from the pen of this author, taking the reader from the devastation of war-torn London to the peace and tranquillity of the Caribbean. As it spans three decades and two continents, Emma experiences love and hatred, rejection and acceptance, and racism that results in heartbreak. It is a story of how staying true to yourself can only lead to the happiness you deserve.

—Carole Cullen, Bilambil Heights, NSW

Skin Deep is a thought-provoking novel by Vera Berry Burrows. This beautiful tale starts in the 1940s and takes you on an exciting journey. We are cleverly transported back and forth in time between England and the Caribbean, as we follow the lives of two young people. A story about taking risks, as Emma, a white secretary, finds love with BJ, a black school teacher. A love story with many obstacles and setbacks as they both try to navigate a society that may not accept their relationship. Will racial differences matter? Is their love strong enough? Are they brave enough? A thoroughly enjoyable read, so set aside some spare time because you won't want to put it down.

—Karen Snowden, Pacific Pines, Gold Coast, Queensland

This is a gentle story of a young Jamaican, BJ Johnson, whose life experiences of injustices, large and small, prepare him for future success. The author skilfully uses the very sensitive theme of racial equality and human rights in a romantic and absorbing manner. Love and separation lead to a creative and subtle mix of the harsh reality of racism combined with feelings of refined sensibility of morals, scruples and family values. Both the English and the Jamaican settings work well to engage the reader. Emma deals with her heartache alone, with continued determination to raise her baby with proper values to become an overall positive thinking human being. The theme of the story goes way beyond the racial parallel to bring together the characters with a freshness, intensity and sensitivity.

—Victoria Seedsman, Clear Island Waters, Queensland.

Dedication

For Sue, always a dear and loyal friend through the ups and the downs, and the highs and the lows, even though we are separated by thousands of miles—thank you.

* * *

One

London – June 1948

The *MV Empire Windrush* arrived at Tilbury Docks carrying four hundred and ninety-two Caribbean passengers, their dark eyes full of expectancy, full of ambition, full of fear of the unknown. Among them was Benjamin Joseph Johnson—BJ to his family and friends. He stared from the gangplank at the hard concrete upon which he was about to place his feet, asking this strange land to accept him. *I'm BJ Johnson,* he silently introduced himself. *I hope I'm the kind of man you are looking for. I'm strong, willing and able to learn any job you want to give me. Please...* Suddenly, his thoughts were interrupted by a strong arm pushing him forward.

"Come on, man. Stop daydreaming and get to the bottom of this ramp."

BJ turned to find a white girl smiling at him. "Sorry, ma'am. I didn't mean to delay you."

The girl shook her head slowly, and still smiling, she nudged him forward again. "I'd like to put my feet on home ground as soon as possible. I've been away far too long. Please…"

BJ quickened his pace as much as the throngs of people ahead of him would allow. He turned to face the girl again and shrugged apologetically. "You'll have to tell *them*," he said, indicating that his fellow passengers didn't seem to understand the need to go faster.

Suddenly, the girl lurched forward, forcing BJ to catch her in order to avoid being floored by a very large, brutish man pushing recklessly through. "Watch out, man!" BJ called, but the guy left them standing in his wake with looks of dismay on their faces. He grinned, a sparkling white, beaming smile. "That's the way to do it," he said as he looked into the eyes of the girl who had unexpectedly fallen into his arms. Feeling suddenly awkward, he eased her away gently, making sure she was on solid ground. Somehow, after only a few seconds, they found themselves stepping off the gangplank onto the jetty.

"Thank you," the girl said.

"Emma! Over here!" were loud cries coming from the right, a short distance away.

Without so much as a smile she was gone, running into the arms of her waiting family. BJ watched as they enveloped her in the obvious love of close relations and momentarily he felt homesick, even before he had hardly set foot in this foreign land. The fear of everything that was alien to him for a moment filled him with dread and desolation. He looked around at the grey buildings that towered above him. A burly guy wearing some kind of uniform and sporting a badge which showed that he was there in an official capacity, ushered BJ and about twenty more dark-faced young men, towards a door marked IMMIGRATION—big black letters on a white background.

"Papers?" another man behind a makeshift desk asked brusquely.

BJ took the documents from his inside pocket and handed them over.

"It says here you're a writer," the man said. "Don't know if you'll earn much here. I doubt there are any jobs that require writers. We want skilled labourers, not arty-farty writers." He smiled at his own attempt at an inappropriate joke.

BJ dared to look to the heavens to hide his embarrassment. "I'll do anything," he said to the still smirking official and keeping his tone amicable. "I'm strong, intelligent, and a quick learner." His thoughts, however, were less than complimentary. *Don't show your ignorance, man. Your country asked for volunteers to help in the workforce. I am a writer, a good writer, but I'll work my butt off to earn a living like most of my compatriots will. Give us a chance, won't you?*

"On your way," the guy instructed, friendly now. "Follow the arrows to the exit and there'll be a charabanc waiting to take you to Clapham South."

"What's at Clapham South?" called a young man who stood a few places behind BJ in the queue. "I hope it's somewhere we'll want to live...you know, clean and comfortable, more suited to humans than dogs." He hunched his shoulders in a pretentious attempt to look taller than his five foot six and strutted with a confidence that belied his diminutive appearance.

All eyes were on the bold, young upstart and BJ tried to signal to him to be quiet. His own expression was one of alarm. *Shut up, man! Jamaicans don't rustle feathers, especially when we stand out like sore thumbs in this sea of white faces. Respect, man. Respect!*

When BJ was on his way to the exit, the young man caught up with him. "What's up with you, man?" he asked belligerently. "We don't bow and scrape to these people. They need us and should acknowledge that fact."

BJ stopped and looked directly into the young man's dark eyes, eyes that were expressively wild. "Calm down, whoever you are..."

"My name is Devon...Devon Harris."

"Well, Devon Harris, you need to show a bit more respect. How old are you?"

"I'm eighteen."

BJ shook his head and stopped to talk. "Ah, so you are young enough to be useful and yet, too young to have enough experience of life for you to take steps in the right direction. You have obviously given coming out here a lot of thought, so you can't be totally ignorant. Just now, we are visitors in this country, and let's face it, we don't exactly blend into the landscape. People will be judging us all the time. *We* know who we are and what we stand for, but they don't know us at all. First impressions and all that they imply must be our mantra."

Devon screwed up his face and looked at the guy who was clearly assessing his character. "What's a mantra? I never came across that word."

"Maybe not, but you need to learn quickly to set a standard for yourself to be recognised as acceptable in whatever you are faced with. Think about it, man. It isn't difficult."

"And who do you think you are, man?" Devon asked indignantly. "I escaped the scrutiny of my parents by coming here. I don't need you to stand in for them. I want to be independent. Why would *I* listen to *you*? Anyway, how old are *you*? You're so full of your own importance, and yet you don't look old enough to have that much experience yourself."

BJ looked with raised eyebrows at his companion. "I'm twenty-eight, but my age doesn't matter, except for the fact I'm older than you," he said. "Don't disrespect your parents, either. I lost my parents when the nineteen forty-four hurricane hit Jamaica. You don't really appreciate their love and affection until it's no longer there. Something needs clarifying here, I think. We both need to know enough about ourselves to make the right choices. In that sense, then yes, we are full of ourselves, that is, full of knowledge about who we are and who we want to be. I just know that drawing attention to yourself can't possibly be good in these circumstances. Take it easy, man! When we are settled and in work, we might be able to prove our worth in other ways. Don't rock the boat! Keep your reputation intact."

"My reputation?" Devon was puzzled.

"What people think of you. I'm trying to tell you that we need to show ourselves in the best light. Shooting your mouth off disrespectfully doesn't exactly do that, does it?"

Devon at least appeared to be momentarily chastened. "Okay, man," he said sullenly. "I'll try. Sorry, man."

BJ slapped him on the back amicably. "You don't have to apologise to me. Come on, let's find this charabanc he was talking about. The sooner we get there, the sooner we'll be able to establish a new life for ourselves."

After an hour waiting for the bus to fill, they set off on the way to their future, a journey into the unknown.

"Onwards and upwards, hey?" Devon said.

BJ grinned. "That's my man! We can do this, Devon Harris."

"Yes, we can," Devon agreed. "Here we go, man."

Two

"Welcome home, my darling girl," the woman said excitedly. "We have missed you so much and look at you! You are so tanned with that Caribbean sun. You must have so much to tell us."

Emma gave her aunt a hug, the second or third since she had run from the gangplank into the welcoming arms of the woman who, five years earlier, had had so many reservations about her niece's decision to travel across the Atlantic in the middle of a war. Five years on, and her thoughts were still confused. *Her father deemed missing in action and her mother, God rest her soul, wasn't here to stop her going away. It was horrific for everybody, especially those who had lived with the threat of being bombed to kingdom come during the London blitz. Now look at our Jack. He hasn't seen his beloved daughter for over six years and I can't be sure he'll even recognise her...*

Emma bent to hug her father. "Hi Dad," she said. "So pleased to see you. I've missed you."

Jack Williams, sitting in a wheelchair, grunted, but said nothing. Emma smiled at him and added, "I'm so, so happy to be home."

~ * ~

It all started one night in late November 1940. Emma had found her mother in the underground air-raid shelter in Hammersmith Station. Although the authorities were not officially giving permission to use the Tube stations as shelters, they closed a blind eye to it and hundreds of Londoners made their way to one station or another as soon as the sirens sounded all around the city. Bunkbeds had been erected in some, and Alice Williams watched and wondered why her neighbour applied copious amounts of cold cream to her face before settling down to sleep. "I'm not going to stop my beauty regime just because Jerry wants to disturb our sleep," she told the curious lady. "At least I'll look good dead if they hit the target!" She laughed raucously and shrugged. "You have to larf," she said seriously. "Otherwise we'd cry, and I'm not letting anybody think I'm scared. We need to stay strong for our men fighting away from home. Keep the home fires burning for when they return." She carried on rubbing the cream into her cheeks, ignoring the stares from the people around her.

When Alice saw Emma pushing through the throngs of people bedding down for as long as German bombers roared overhead, she directed angry words at her daughter from a distance. "Emma Williams, where have you been? I've been out of my mind with worry. I thought you hadn't heard the siren—"

"Mother," Emma scolded. "I'm eighteen! I'm almost an adult. I can look after myself. Please don't worry when I'm not by your side all the time. You have to let me grow up sometime. I can't always be tied to your apron strings."

"There's a war on, you silly girl," her mother continued. "I'm bound to worry. It's hard enough with your father fighting at the Front. I'm on edge all the time thinking about what's happening to him without you adding to my stress."

Emma hugged her mother and kissed her on the cheek. "Sorry," she whispered. "I didn't mean to worry you, but I've been talking to—" She stopped abruptly. Her mind was in overdrive. *Not now,* she told herself silently. *I need Mother in a good frame of mind when I tell her about my plans.*

~ * ~

Earlier that evening, she had been dancing at the Hammersmith Palais de Danse, the only place open for people, especially young people, to escape the misery of what was happening all around them. Soldiers on leave went there, too. Emma loved chatting to them about their lives, even though some of them just used the opportunity to unburden themselves of experiences they were trying to forget. Mostly, they were proud of what they had done and were prepared for what was to come. On that particular evening, she had been asked to dance by a chief petty officer who was on leave from his posting on *HMS Nabob*.

"Obviously, I can't make any plans for myself just now," he told Emma when she asked if he had any plans for after the war. "But I know what I'd be doing if I were a civilian. I'd try to take myself off to Jamaica, or the Cayman Islands. It's as safe there as you can be these days, and there are jobs available if you are prepared to look around."

"Wouldn't you join the Home Guard if you were unfit for active service?" Emma asked. "I couldn't imagine any man would want to leave the country while its people needed them on the Home Front."

"Is that your way of telling me off?" he asked. "Well, maybe I would, but I have no family here," he explained. "My ex-wife went to New Zealand with her new partner and, co-incidentally, war broke out soon after she left." He shrugged and grinned. "There's a joke in there somewhere!"

Emma smiled. "Tell me more about the Caribbean and Jamaica, since you mentioned it before," she urged. "It sounds very interesting."

"Jamaican politics have been in disarray for a while, but some trade union guy is in charge now and, from all accounts, he's doing a decent job. Mind you, I can tell you for certain that the Jamaica I have seen is beautiful and I believe they need people to do specific jobs. You'd have to enquire about that. They have a comparatively small population. Many of the men have joined up and have gone to Trinidad or the United States to train."

"So it can't be as safe as you are making it sound...I mean, are people safe in their homes? I saw a movie once set in Jamaica, and the locals were breaking into white folks' houses and looting and stealing," Emma offered guardedly. "Are they all…" she paused, her face suddenly feeling hot. She was embarrassed at what she was about to ask.

As if he were telepathic, her dancing partner answered. "Black people?"

She nodded.

"Well," he said, "There is a big British and European influence in their history, so there are white people over there, but Jamaica is a Caribbean island which makes it synonymous with black people. They were taken to work on the plantations during…Well, I'm sure you know when, but is that a problem for you?"

Emma looked at him directly. "No, not at all; certainly not for me personally, but it's still a delicate subject with a lot of people these days. Anyway, how do you know all this? I'd love to do something different. In spite of the war, I do believe there are opportunities somewhere in the world apart from joining the land army or working in the munitions factories here in England."

"I actually found all this out from a Jamaican guy on the *Nabob*. He was coming over here to enlist. He was very knowledgeable and had it all worked out for when the war is over. I couldn't understand why he wanted to come here to join up, but there you go. That's his business, not mine. In my opinion, going overseas would be the way to go," he said. "But I'm speaking out of turn even telling you all this. What would your parents say? If you are serious about doing something different, you have to understand that going across the Atlantic is still not completely safe, but it's a lot safer than going in the opposite direction." He paused and took a deep breath. "I know I shouldn't be encouraging you to leave home, but…well, that's what I'd do until the war is over."

"Sounds wonderful," she enthused. "I think I might look into it." The music ended and the CPO escorted her back to her seat near her friend, Mavis, who had watched on as Emma waltzed around the floor with her handsome sailor.

"Thanks for the dance," he said. "See you around."

Emma smiled. "Yeah, maybe."

"Hmm?" Mavis grinned. "He looked nice. How come you've let him walk off?"

"Mavis!" Emma scolded. "I've told you before I'm not looking for a boyfriend. What would be the point? They all go off to war and it's unlikely we'd ever see them again." She nudged her friend playfully. "Let's just enjoy ourselves; no strings attached."

The music started up again and a very handsome young soldier whom Emma assumed was an American GI was standing in front of her. "Beautiful young lady," he asked, his request delivered with genuine charm. "May I have this dance?"

Emma beamed back. "How could I refuse such a lovely request?" He took her hand and led her to the middle of the dance floor as Mavis got up to dance with his mate.

The boogie-woogie beat had them tapping their feet and swing dancing with happy abandon. "Gee, you sure can dance, Miss," he complimented.

Emma grinned. "Only when I have a good partner," she replied between twists and turns and snappy foot movements that completely complemented those of her partner.

"We should do this more often," he said. "I have never had a girl dance so well with me. We were made for each other."

Emma laughed out loud. "I bet you say that to all the girls, you smooth talker. I've heard all about you GIs. What's your name?"

"I'm Wayne, and you might have heard about GIs, but I'm Canadian, not American and I'm not in the army. I'm in the RCAF and a rear gunner. I have a few days' leave before I need to go back to the base in North Yorkshire, but you really are a good dancer." He laughed with her as the honky-tonk music came to an end.

"Thanks and sorry about dropping a clanger," Emma said. "But you all sound the same to me."

"Not if you got a Yank and a Canadian together," he explained. "And the Yanks haven't joined the war up to now, unless you have some inside information that hasn't reached the rest of us yet. I think they don't want the big bills war always brings."

"Really?" Emma was surprised. "Is it all about money?"

Wayne shrugged. "That's what we mere mortals think, but I'm not sure that's the real reason. They are so far away from what's going on in Europe..."

"But so are the Canadians," Emma reminded him.

"Yes, but we're part of the Commonwealth and there's the difference in a nutshell."

At ten o'clock, there was a long drum roll and everybody stood to attention while the national anthem was played. Wayne, who had stayed with Emma since their first dance asked, "May I walk you home, Miss Emma? It's not safe to be walking the streets alone at this time of night and there's a war on, you know?"

"Away with you," she told him. "I just live a couple of blocks away so I'll be fine." But the sirens blared as she bid him a swift goodbye and ran to where she knew her mother would be in the Hammersmith Tube station. Wayne watched as she ran off down the Fulham Road, stuck his hands in his pockets and walked off in the opposite direction to find his own safe place while the Germans were flying overhead.

~ * ~

The next evening, Emma went to the Palais hoping to see the Navy guy again and find out more about going overseas away from the bombs and all that the war had thrust upon them. "Please don't stay out too long," her mother begged, completely oblivious of Emma's plans for the future. "I do worry when you aren't with me."

"I won't," the girl replied. "And don't worry. I have my gasmask and I'm wearing flat shoes so I can run to the Underground and find you if there's another air-raid."

"Nothing's so sure," her mother told her sagely. "It's been every night for the past week. We are lucky our house is still standing. I do wonder for how long..."

"Mother!" Emma chastised. "Stop all this nonsense. I was born to survive and so were you. Anyway, I'm looking at some means of getting us to a safe haven for the rest of the war. I'll tell you about it when I know more myself."

Alice Williams forced a half smile for her daughter as she bid her goodbye, but her thoughts were full of fear and dread. *Safe haven indeed...silly girl! How can she be so optimistic when the world is going mad around us? I know she's young and ambitious, but I can't entertain any thoughts for the future. I have this same feeling every time the sirens go off. Something is going to happen, I just know it; I feel it in my bones. Keep safe, my precious child.* She picked up her knitting and told herself she was helping the war effort by joining the *Knit Socks for Soldiers* initiative. The wireless crackled into life and Wilfred Pickles was reading the news. An Allied invasion of Sicily and Italy followed the success in North Africa and Mussolini's government had fallen. Alice smiled to herself. *Thank the Lord for that,* she thought. *Surely the Tommies can get the better of the Jerries. I have every faith in my Jack. He'll never give up, I know that—*

Without warning, the walls shook and the whole building bore the brunt of the enemy's incendiary bombs. Within seconds, Alice was gone. As the sirens blared *after* the catastrophic event, those who were able, ran for their lives into the shelters, jumping over debris and hurdling what was left of garden gates before, they presumed, the second round of bombs would drop from a sky already heavily laden with smoke and choking smog from the devastation created by the German bombardment.

Emma was in the Palais when the first bombs dropped. The dancing stopped and the revellers instinctively looked up at the vaulted ceiling decorated with gold painted coving and elaborate chandeliers that shook in defiance of Hitler's attack. Instinctively, and seemingly in slow motion, the dancers moved swiftly in silence to hide under tables and chairs, huddling together and holding on tight to comparative strangers. There was none of the usual screaming and shouting, no cries for help, just an eerie silence until hearts were beating at a normal rate again and people began to whisper furtively as if the enemy were actually trying to listen in to what they were saying.

The Canadian gunner, Wayne, who had sought out Emma early in the evening, held her close and tried to calm her nerves. She was shaking violently and he whispered in her ear, "You're all right, Emma.

I've got you. As soon as we hear the all clear, we'll get out of this place and I'll take you home."

Emma shook her head. "No, I must go to the Tube station. Mum will be there and she'll be worried. I'm going to get her away from all this. She needs to know as soon as possible that I'm okay. She'll be waiting for me. I'm going now—"

Mavis had run to Emma's side as soon as the building shuddered from the blast and the three of them huddled together under a small table that was just big enough to give them makeshift protection.

"You can't go yet," Wayne told her firmly. "If the second wave comes, you won't stand a chance out there."

Mavis agreed. "Calm down, Em. You know as well as I do that your mum will be safe in the shelter. What's the point of putting yourself at risk?"

"But she'll be worried about me, I know that for a fact," Emma cried. "I have to be with her."

Wayne held her hand tightly. "Just wait until the all clear comes and I promise I'll personally make sure you find your mom." He looked into the fearful eyes of the girl who just moments ago was laughing and joking as they danced together. "I promise," he said again, and they remained huddled under the table.

Three

BJ and Devon watched the English countryside flash by as they sat in the charabanc in silence. The seats were full of men with black faces, all whose eyes showed a mixture of excitement, curiosity and fear. Devon looked at BJ and whispered, "Look at those houses. They are dark and miserable and all joined together in a row. It's June, and there's no sun. What are we letting ourselves in for?"

"It's certainly different from what we've left behind," BJ agreed. "I don't know anybody here, so I have no chance of living with an already established Jamaican family like some of the guys I was travelling with, and I assume you are in the same boat."

Devon nodded. "I'm already wondering if I have done the right thing. It took me ages to save up the twenty-eight pounds for the passage and my sister saved up the other five pounds we had to have to bring with us."

BJ sighed. "I saved up enough to see me through for a few weeks," he said. "I'm hoping I find work very quickly. I'll sweep streets if necessary until I can find more meaningful employment."

"I've no idea what I'll do," Devon admitted. "I was working with my daddy on the plantation. My granddaddy was given some land after emancipation and because the sugar industry was mainly taken over by Tate and Lyle, my granddaddy turned his hand to growing bananas. It gave us a living, but we were always quite poor. I guess there'll be no jobs for banana growers here." He shrugged and sighed resignedly.

"There'll be something for a young, strong man like you," BJ reassured him.

"I hope so," Devon replied. "I certainly hope so."

The charabanc eased to a stop outside what looked like a train station. They found a reception tent at the top of the entrance to what had been used as a shelter during the war. Devon looked wide-eyed at his new friend and then looked down the deep, dark shaft. "Looks like I was right about our living quarters," he said. "I wouldn't keep a dog down there."

"Don't judge it until we've seen it," BJ advised. "At least we will have somewhere to rest our heads at night..." He was interrupted by a lady in a green uniform thrusting a clean white sheet and a grey blanket at him. "Name?"

"BJ Johnson."

"Bunk number ten," she said, and, picking up another sheet and blanket for Devon, she continued, "Name?"

"Devon Harris."

"Bunk number twelve."

"Can't I be next to him?" Devon asked, confirming he was with BJ.

"You *are* next to him," she told him. "Even numbers are side by side. Both top bunks and next to the privy."

"And that's good, is it?" Devon asked, the rebellious trait in his character raising its ugly head again.

"You'll think so when you need to go in the middle of the night," the woman said dismissively. "Next!"

BJ grabbed Devon's arm and pulled him into the shaft before he could start world war three. "Calm down, man. Let's see what it's like first. Beggars can't be choosers and we have to be grateful we have a bed and are out of this cold weather that is supposed to be the British summer."

"But it's like being in a prison," Devon grumbled.

"How would you know that?" BJ asked. "Don't tell me you've been inside."

"No, I haven't," Devon assured him. "I would never have been accepted if I had. I might be outspoken, but I'm not a criminal."

"Thank the good Lord for that," BJ said. "Phew! You had me worried there for a moment. Here we are, numbers ten and twelve, and side by side as the lovely lady said." He pressed on the pillow already on the bed. "Not too bad," he commented. "We'll manage for a few days."

"Do you always look on the bright side?" Devon asked him.

"I try to," BJ replied. "I see exactly what you see…the poorly lit, clammy, musty tunnels offered to us as suitable accommodation. They are primitive and unwelcoming, but we are in a strange new land that itself is recovering from six years of war, so we have to accept what's on offer…"

Devon regarded him with respect. "You are a good guy, BJ Johnson. Pleased to have made your acquaintance."

BJ smiled. "It will only be temporary accommodation, you'll see," he said. "Right now, we have very few alternatives, if any at all."

That evening, they were ushered into the food marquee where they were served a lavish meal of roast beef, Yorkshire pudding, potatoes, green vegetables and gravy followed by suet pudding with currants and custard. For six shillings and sixpence a day, they had a bed and three hot meals. Suitably fed, they returned to their bunks and slept soundly in preparation for the job-hunting they would have to do during the coming days.

~ * ~

After a few good nights' sleep and nourishing breakfasts, BJ set off to the Employment Exchange with a number of other men from the shelter. Devon loitered behind and helped the girl in the food marquee to clear away breakfast and set up for lunch.

"You're a born waiter," the girl told him. "Why don't you go and find out what jobs are available in hotels? It would be a good start for you."

"Oh, I don't know about that," Devon said nervously. "Who would want a black person serving their food? I'm very wary about putting myself out there. I don't mind admitting that."

The girl stopped what she was doing and walked up to Devon who was setting out the cutlery on the next table. "Look," she said quietly. "I know what you are saying, and there are people out there who would be suspicious of you, but if you show that you can work hard without rocking the boat—"

Devon smiled. "You aren't the first person to tell me that in the last couple of days."

"Oh? And who else would give you that piece of advice?"

"My new friend, BJ. If you'd heard me when we first arrived, you wouldn't even be talking to me now."

"Why not?"

"Because I was so loud and objectionable as soon as I stepped onto dry land. I embarrassed BJ and I embarrassed myself," Devon admitted. "I expected everybody to call me *Boy* as some white people still did in Jamaica, so I stood up for myself before they were able to treat me as inferior. I was really cocky. I thought I was showing my superiority, but BJ put me straight."

"Oh my goodness," the girl cried. "I thought all that business was done. I'm so sorry...What's your name? *I'd* like to know who I'm talking to."

"I'm Devon; Devon Harris. And you are?"

"I'm Rose," she said, "but if I tell you my surname, promise me you won't laugh."

Devon grinned. "That bad, hey? No, I won't laugh, I promise."

"Waddle."

Devon was puzzled. "Why do you want me to waddle?" he asked, but he bent his knees and waddled away from her like a duck.

"There you go!" Rose exclaimed. "You're making fun of me already."

Devon was aghast. "Wha gwaan?"

Rose started laughing. "What does that mean? Speak English, please."

Devon was confused. "What does what mean?"

"What you said...wha gw...?"

"Oh that. It means what's up or what's going on, in the King's English. We Jamaicans say it all the time. Nobody ever questioned the way I speak. I'll have to try to be more English, I guess, if I want people to understand me. Can't do much about the accent, though," he replied amicably. "Why did you say I was making fun of you? *You* were making fun of *me* asking me to walk like a duck!"

Now they were laughing together, hitting each other playfully in turn. Rose stopped first. "My name is Rose Waddle," she explained and waited for Devon's reaction.

"Oh," he said sombrely, but the urge to laugh was too great for them both and they fell about laughing again until they were both breathless.

"Well, that's got that over with," Rose announced cheerily. "So are you going to the Employment Exchange or what?"

"What?" Devon said and then they laughed again. "I'll go when we've finished here."

"Would you like me to go with you?" Rose asked. "I will, you know, if you want me to."

"Yeah, that'd be just fine. Thank you, Rose."

~ * ~

BJ wore his best light grey pin-striped suit for his interview with the Employment Officer. He waited quietly, nervous about what they might ask him. *Do I look smart enough for them? Will my qualifications be accepted here? Will they question the validity of my certificates? My papers say I was educated in a British based school. Surely that will count for something.*

"Benjamin Johnson?" the officer called out. "Come this way."

BJ stood straight, tipped his new trilby hat before he removed it, and followed the gentleman into an office. He waited until he was asked to take a seat and then sat stiffly upright opposite the officer who placed BJ's papers on the desk in front of him. "You can relax, sir," he advised and then with a wry smile, "I'm William Blake...not *the* William Blake, of course."

BJ was taken aback. *He called me sir!* "Thank you, Mr Blake," he said and he physically allowed his muscles to rest easy without appearing too casual. In an effort to make himself feel more comfortable, he took a deep breath and added to Mr Blake's previous little joke. "I love your work, sir, particularly *The Tyger*."

There was a long silence in the room and BJ's thoughts were troubled. *Oh my goodness. I've said the wrong thing. I've been too familiar. How stupid can I be mentioning* The Tyger? *I could have quoted some other works of William Blake other than that which is so full of controversy.*

Then the clerk looked up and smiled. "You are very well qualified, Mr Johnson. I don't think manual work would be your forte."

"I'll do anything, sir. I'm strong and fit and I'm a quick learner."

"I can appreciate all that, but I know there will be something more appropriate to your academic qualifications. You might like to consider becoming a teacher in one of our primary schools. Would you agree?"

BJ was shocked. "But I don't have a teaching qualification," he admitted.

"Don't you worry about that just now," Bill Blake said. "We have initiatives in place for such as you—well educated, well-spoken and very knowledgeable, from all accounts." He winked. "We won't get into a discussion about *The Tyger*. Maybe another time."

"Thank you, sir," a relieved BJ said, smiling in acknowledgement of Mr Blake's acceptance of his *faux pas*.

"We'll be in touch soon, Mr Johnson. Welcome to England. I hope we can give you all that you are looking for. Good morning, sir."

"Good morning, Mr Blake, and thank you."

Four

For what seemed like hours, Emma, Mavis and Wayne sheltered under the table at the edge of the dance floor. When the all clear sounded, they scrambled from their makeshift shelter and made for the door. Everybody walked at a steady pace and Wayne placed an arm around each girl in a bold effort to make them feel secure.

"I'll leave you two now," Mavis announced. "I live in the opposite direction from Emma."

"Are you sure you'll be all right?" Emma asked. "Wayne can go with you. I know I'll find Mum in the Hammersmith shelter, so at least I know she'll be safe."

"No, let Wayne go with you. I'll be fine," Mavis urged. "My dad's on leave so he'll have looked after Mum and the kids. They'll all be in the cellar at the pub." She smiled weakly. "See yer later, Em."

"Okay, Maeve. So long as you're sure."

Wayne took Emma's hand. "Lead the way," he said. "I'll stay with you until you find your mom."

Emma smiled. "Your accent makes me laugh," she told him. "You say mom, and I say mum. It's a bit like tomato/tomarto, isn't it? It would be logical for us to say potarto, wouldn't it?"

"You are so cute," he commented, shaking his head slowly. "We can have the pronunciation discussion later. Come on, let's find your mom *and* your mum. How far down the Fulham Road is it?"

"It's not far. Just a couple of blocks..." She stopped abruptly and looked down the road as far as the eye could see. "Oh, my good lord," she cried and set off running towards the mounds of smoking rubble before her. "Oh my god! Mother? Mother? Please God, let her still be in the shelter." She turned and looked at Wayne who was following her as she ran. Her eyes were wild and full of unshed tears. "I'm scared, Wayne. That pile of rubble just there where somebody's gas stove is poking through the bricks...that's the end of our street. I can't even see the road to the shelter. It's all gone!"

Wayne tried to calm her with gentle, positive words of hope. "Even if the houses are gone, the shelter will still be safe. Don't think the worst. We'll find your mom and let her know you are okay. Please, Emma. Try not to think of the worst-case scenario."

Emma was in tears. "I can't help it," she sobbed.

Suddenly she spotted old Mrs Blackshaw who lived four doors down from Emma and her mum. The old lady was poking through the rubble with her walking stick. "Have you seen my mum?" she asked.

Mrs Blackshaw looked up with sad eyes. "I haven't, dearie. She wasn't in the shelter. I managed to get down there 'cos I was walking past the entrance when I heard the bombers. I don't know why the sirens didn't go off...and look at our houses; blown to bits. What are we going to do now?" She looked at Emma as though she expected her to provide the answer.

Emma sank to her knees and sobbed into her hands. "No, no, no!" she cried. "Not my mum..." Instinctively, she stood and moved to where she thought her house had stood and frantically began to dig into the rubble with her bare hands. Wayne helped as best he could until he could find no valid reason to carry on.

"Emma," he said quietly. "We can't do this. The authorities are just a bit further along from here. They have the equipment and the right tools. They'll carry on digging until they find..."

Emma stood to face him. "Until what, Wayne? Until they find my mum's body? I have to keep digging. Mum might be hurt, and I'll need to get her to the hospital if it's still standing. I hate those bastard Germans..." And she wept openly until the Auxiliary Fire Service removed much of the shattered buildings, listening all the time for any signs of life. The whole procedure was futile. There wasn't a cat in hell's chance of finding anybody alive in the devastating destruction of the life they had always known, a life shattered by faceless individuals who randomly wiped out innocent people.

The following day, Wayne returned to his North Yorkshire base and she never saw him again.

~ * ~

Emma went to stay with her aunt, her father's sister in Windsor. She had been traumatised by the horrific death of her mother and while she recuperated in relative safety, Auntie Edith had looked after her. Each morning she had a cup of tea in bed and a slice of bread sparsely covered with strawberry spread made with fruit from her aunt's garden. Slowly the colour reappeared in her cheeks and with regular walks in Windsor Great Park when the weather was pleasantly mild, she began to feel well again.

Edith Booth had welcomed her niece into her home. Her husband, Leonard, had been an aeronautical meteorologist serving as a military attaché overseas and had been one of the first casualties of the war when Germany bombed Norway. At the time of her sister-in-law's death, Edith had needed a worthwhile distraction from her prolonged grief and she delighted in caring for Emma.

Emma stayed there until June 1943, helping with daily chores, serving in the soup kitchen that had been set up to help those who didn't have gardens to grow their own vegetables and also finding opportunities for those same people to find allotments so they, too, might help to feed themselves and others. One bright summer evening, Emma sat in the garden with her aunt and watched as the sun set in the west.

"Look how beautiful that is," she commented. "You wouldn't know there was a war on but for the nasty memories we have that never seem to go away."

"No, dear, we wouldn't, but sadly, we have to go on as best we can," her aunt replied. "Are you feeling all right, Emma? You seem to be very melancholy."

"Yes, I'm fine," Emma said," but…"

"But what?" Auntie Edith asked, dubious of her niece's frame of mind.

"Just before Mum died, I met a sailor at the Palais, and he was telling me about the West Indies. It has been foremost in my mind recently. He said if he were a civilian, he would go to Jamaica or the Cayman Islands to find a bit of peace and get away from bombs dropping every night…"

"That's silly," Aunt Edith scoffed. "Here we are in Windsor, and the bombs have been stopped for ages now. Hitler realised he couldn't win the war across the English Channel, so he started to concentrate on Russia. Only time will tell where that will lead him. We have to hope he's too ambitious for his own good."

"I know all that," Emma stated, "but I am seriously thinking about trying it over there and seeing if what he said is true. He painted a very pretty picture."

"You are what?" her aunt gasped. "Don't be ridiculous, Emma."

"I'm not being ridiculous, Auntie. My dad is missing and we've had no news from the Foreign Office for ages. To all intents and purposes, I'm an orphan…a war orphan, and I'm going to take control of my life."

"Please dear, think carefully about this," Edith advised. "There are still U-boats in the Atlantic and it can't possibly be safe. It's madness for you even to consider such a journey. I read somewhere that the crime rate over there is horrendous. You'll be at the mercy of criminals as well as worrying about what is happening because of the war. Whatever are you thinking?"

"I'm thinking I could do something more meaningful with my life..."

"What can be more meaningful than looking after your fellow man? I thought you were happy here helping our friends."

Emma sighed. "I'm not unhappy, Auntie, but I long to be away from here, no disrespect to you. I appreciate all you have done for me, but I am still young and in spite of the war still going on, I have to spread my wings and achieve something besides mooching around Windsor day after day."

Edith stared at her niece with sad eyes. "I don't know what to say, Emma. What do you mean *mooching* around Windsor?"

"You know what my days entail, Auntie. I get up, I walk to the park, I serve at the soup kitchen and then by three o'clock in the afternoon, I'm done. I've read all your books, most of them twice and I feel I'm not really achieving anything. Establishing myself in a new place would provide me with a challenge. I know I can be useful to somebody over there."

"Well, you are twenty-one now and officially an adult. In that respect, you can make your own decisions, but what happens when your dad comes home and you're not here?"

"Don't you mean *if* he comes home?" Emma corrected. "I know there's a war on and that's why I need to do something *now*; not next year; not when the war is over. How do we know what's going to happen to us? Great Britain might not be so great if Hitler has his way."

Edith sighed. "I can't believe you are giving up on your country on a whim," she said bluntly. "All the news points to the allies defeating the Nazis. With America in with us now, it will all be over sooner rather than later. Please reconsider your decision, Emma. Please."

Emma sighed, too. "I'm trying to find out as much as I can about going to Jamaica. I'm checking the merchant ships which cross the Atlantic regularly as hospital and supply vessels. I'll work my passage if possible."

"That's all well and good, but what will you do when you arrive in Jamaica? You'll have nowhere to live; no job, and you won't know anybody. Can't you see how foolish this is?" Edith could think of nothing more to convince Emma that she was being foolhardy. "Don't you see that you are making a very selfish decision?"

Emma was taken aback. "I don't think I'm being selfish, Auntie. I'm going to work in a place that needs people like me. I've researched what jobs will be available and I might be able to become a nanny to children of plantation owners—"

"Stop!" Edith cried. "How can you even think about such a position? Those people buy other less fortunate people as slaves. And you'll stick out like a sore thumb amongst a sea of black faces. How do you know those black people are like us? I'm appalled. Please don't do it, Emma. Your mother will turn in her grave."

"Don't you dare bring my mother into this," Emma said more scathingly than necessary. "It's three years since she died, and even then I was planning to take her over there to get her out of the Blitz. I was going to tell her the night she..." She took a deep breath in an attempt to prevent the tears coming again. "She would have supported me in anything I decided to do; I just know she would. And there are no slaves in this day and age, Auntie. Emancipation happened in 1834 and that's more than a hundred years ago. Strange though it may seem to you, I researched that as well."

"There's no need to use that sarcastic tone with me, Emma," Edith told her firmly. "I've stated my case to make you think about changing your mind, but I can see in your eyes that you are determined to go regardless of what I think. You are indeed your father's daughter. He was always the same, obstinate, if the truth be known. Please keep me informed of your plans." With that, Edith walked away, leaving Emma looking as guilty as a child caught with her hand in the biscuit box.

The letter she left for Auntie Edith said what she wanted to explain but hadn't been able to vocalise. The atmosphere at home hadn't been great during the preparations for her trip, but she knew she had to put her feelings in writing for the woman who had looked after her when she needed it most.

Dear Auntie Edith,

I didn't want to upset you, but it's clear that I have. I hope you will understand my need to leave this place and find solace in the sun with people who from all accounts are happier than people here who have had their spirits bombed out of them. I would never have known about Jamaica but for my Royal Navy acquaintance, but he sounded so enthusiastic about the place he had visited even when the war was going on all around him. I'm young and free, and my spirit of adventure is burning brightly in my heart. Please be happy for me.

I promise to keep in touch as much as I am able and yes, I do know there's a war still going on, but hopefully some mail will get through on the supply ships.

The ship I'm going on as a galley hand will be part of a convoy of Liberty ships made in the United States from a British idea. I'm sure you'll have read all about them in The Times. There will mainly be Jamaican and American soldiers on board who have been injured, but also people like me who are eager to travel the high seas and be of good use to anybody who needs them. I feel so strongly that I'm going where I'm needed. Call it Fate or intuition, but I instinctively know it's right.

Please remember that I am old enough to look after myself and I won't have my head turned by any GI with an eye for the ladies. That's a joke, Auntie! Don't be looking for things to worry about. I'm not searching for a boyfriend or soulmate or whatever else you want to call such a male companion.

Take care, dear Auntie. I love you and I'll be back when I have satisfied my inner craving for adventure.

Emma xx

PS Please let me know if you receive news of Dad. I don't hold out much hope, but I'll want to know whatever the news might be.

Five

The voyage to Jamaica began as soon as the ship left Southampton, but leaving British waters was an experience Emma would prefer to forget. As soon as they hit the Bay of Biscay, the comparatively small troopship seemed to be tossed around, making stomachs lurch and faces turn green at the gills.

"This is just the practice for when we reach the Atlantic," the captain said. "You'll be fine when your stomach has adjusted to the roll of the ship. Give it a few days and you'll be able to add your skills of coping in the galley of a ship in rough seas to your resumé. Mark my words, it will be a feather in your cap!"

The ship stopped in the port of Gibraltar to pick up supplies, re-fuel and accept any military personnel who needed to be transported across the Atlantic. The crew weren't allowed to go ashore, even though General Eisenhower had taken command of operations there after the successful campaigns in North Africa, and the surrender of Italy earlier that year.

Emma had waited with sheer dread for the time they would be sailing westwards from Gibraltar and crossing the invisible line into the Atlantic Ocean proper, but once they were there, just as the captain had said, she felt she had gained her sea legs and went about her galley duties with renewed confidence. Some of the bed-confined soldiers weren't so lucky, and she found herself comforting and caring for the more vulnerable of them. It seemed to shorten the days for them and for her. At night, when in her tiny berth, she chatted to her new friend and galley mate, who slept in the bunk above her.

"Why are you going to Jamaica, Ann?" she asked.

Ann didn't answer right away. "Can I trust you to keep a secret? I mean, I've only just met you and, even though we clicked straight away, I'm not sure I can tell you just yet."

Emma was oddly puzzled. "Blimey, that sounds mysterious, but it was just a casual question and you don't have to tell me." She was trying to keep her tone friendly. "Please don't think I'm being nosy." She paused to sense what Ann's reaction was going to be and then to lighten the atmosphere, "It isn't easy, you know, talking to a mattress above my head. Do you want to come down and sit with me? I'll go to the galley and make us a cup of tea if you like."

"Sounds good," Ann said cheerily, and she swung her legs over the side of the bunk, catching Emma off guard and kicking her on the back of her head. "Oh gawd, I'm so sorry," Ann wailed.

Emma laughed. "I'm okay," she assured her friend. "It'll take more than a little tap on my head to floor me." She rubbed her head playfully. "I'll live," she announced and went down to the galley to make the tea. When she returned with two mugs of steaming tea, she handed one to Ann and then sat next to her on the bed.

It was Ann's suggestion that they talk.

Emma patted Ann on the knee. "You don't have to tell me anything if you choose not to," she said amicably. "We are both leaving the land of our birth in the middle of a stupid war and that in itself is enough for other people to question our decisions. Personally, I don't care what other people think. It's my life, my decision. If it's a mistake, then it's my mistake and I'll sort it."

"I wish I could think like that," Ann said. "I do feel guilty that I've left my family all because I fell in love. The authorities don't know I'm following my lover to Jamaica. He was shipped home last month and I miss him so much and—"

Emma looked at the girl and saw complete confusion in her eyes. "What's wrong, Ann? I think I'd be happy to be following the man of my dreams. Up to now, I haven't found him, not that I've been looking."

"Well, my family really sent me packing. I'm pregnant, you see."

"Oh," was all Emma could say.

"Not only that, I'm pregnant with a mixed-race child."

"Oh."

"Please say something more than *oh,* Em. If truth be known, I'm scared witless."

Emma took Ann's hand and held it tightly. Looking directly into her eyes, she thought before she spoke. "I'm not really in a position to give advice about this situation, but what's done is done. Does your fella know about the baby?"

Ann shook her head. "He'd gone before I could tell him. I really don't know what he'll think."

"Well, think of the positives. When he knows, he'll want you to be with him—"

Ann took a sharp intake of breath. "He doesn't know I'm coming either. I didn't tell him because I didn't want to tell him in the first letter I wrote to him. When dad told me never to darken his door again, I just went to the docks in Southampton and registered with the Liberty ships agent. They had a notice saying they needed galley hands so I thought my ship had come in." She grinned. "Pardon the pun."

"Oh goodness!" Emma exclaimed. "That puts a different slant on things, doesn't it? You know where he lives then?"

"I do. Earl gave me his address before he left. He lives in a place called Spanish Town. I'll have to get a taxi when we land and then hope he's pleased to see me."

"I'm sure he will be," Emma said, presuming she wasn't giving Ann false hope. "He loved you enough to get you pregnant, so..."

"Emma!" Ann exclaimed laughing. "That's a sweeping statement. All men like a bit of hanky-panky; they wouldn't be normal if they didn't. It doesn't always say they love you. Sex is a conquest to them. I know, believe me."

Emma was wide-eyed. "I've got to say I wouldn't know anything about that sort of thing..."

"Didn't you meet any randy servicemen then?" Ann asked with a glint in her eye.

"Maybe I did at Hammersmith Palais, but I didn't let them hang around long enough to try it on. I danced with them and then danced with the next guy." She thought about the night her house was blasted to kingdom come with her mother in it. "I did meet a nice Canadian gunner. He helped me when my house was bombed in the blitz. He hung around for a while, but then he went back to his base in North Yorkshire and I had to go to Windsor to live with my aunt," she explained. "I guess I could have liked him if I'd had the chance to take it further. I don't know if I'd have slept with him, though."

"You are very virtuous, aren't you? I wish I'd been the same," Ann said wistfully. "Every time I met a soldier, especially the GIs during the last couple of years, I told myself I might be giving him his last bit of pleasure before he had to go and fight at the Front. I knew most of them would think I was easy, but I didn't care. I was doing my bit for the war effort!" She giggled girlishly and Emma joined in.

"But what about Earl?" she asked. "Was he different from the others?"

"I think he was," Ann revealed. "He said he loved me and none of the others ever did. He was gentle and quietly spoken. It wasn't just sex with him, it was making love. I think that's why I got pregnant 'cos I was more relaxed...you know, it wasn't just a quickie up against the wall with him. He held me close and stroked my hair afterwards and said he loved me over and over again."

"It sounds like you've found Mr Right, doesn't it?" Emma said. "Like I said before, look on the bright side. At least you have somewhere to go when you leave the ship. I have no idea what I'll do or where I'll go. I'm just hoping I can find a nice little hotel for a few days while I sort myself out."

"You're very brave, Em," Ann told her.

"So are you, Ann." Emma insisted. "We are both going on a journey into the unknown, but you know, I feel it's right. I can't explain it, but it just feels right."

~ * ~

They arrived in Kingston, Jamaica, just short of four weeks after they left Southampton. The Atlantic had proved to be a gentle giant. It had been calm and enjoyable for the most part, especially on deck where Emma felt the sea air filling her lungs and the stiff breeze blowing through her blonde hair. Rumours of U-boats patrolling those waters were exactly that, just rumours, although the junior petty officer confirmed that the Battle of the Atlantic had made it comparatively safe for them to cross without much danger. The glorious Allies now had control of the great ocean British people call the Pond.

Disembarking provided both girls with mixed feelings. "I'll miss you," Ann told Emma as they hugged affectionately.

"I'll miss you too, but try and keep in touch, won't you?" Emma said firmly.

"I will, and here's Earl's address." She handed Emma a slip of paper. "If you are stuck, just turn up. I'm sure he'll help."

With that, they hugged one last time and, as Emma went out of Immigration to walk to the bed and breakfast place she had been told about, Ann went to the taxi rank for the trip to Spanish Town and Earl's house, whatever it might hold.

Six

Emma walked south for about fifteen minutes in the direction of the city and searched for the small bed and breakfast place situated down a winding sandy track just off the main street. Hot and breathless, she stopped and looked in awe at the view. *Wow!* she thought. *That sailor boy was right. It is so beautiful and so untouched, especially by German bombs.* Ahead of her was white sand and turquoise blue ocean, something she had only ever seen in pictures. Suddenly, a couple of teenage boys ran around the bend in the track and stopped by her side as they greeted her. "Hi there, mamma. You need help?"

Emma was startled. "Oh...er...erm...I'm looking for The Shack," she told them. "Am I going the right way?"

The smaller of the two boys grinned. "Whey u a seh, mamma?"

Emma looked completely puzzled until the older of the two spoke. "Elliot, watch yo' manners. She not Yardie."

"Please, can't you speak English?" she begged.

The boys laughed. "Sorry mamma. We not used to dem foreigners coming here," the older boy explained. "Shack just down here on the left and dat der in front of you is the beach."

"Thank you," Emma replied. "It's lovely."

"It's lovely," Elliot mimicked, but the older boy rapped his arm. "Wha yuh deh pon, Joseph?"

"We know English, Elliot, so speak it to the lady."

Elliot appeared to be contrite. "Sorry, mamma. I not mean disrespect."

"That's okay," she replied. "I do stand out..." She stopped abruptly. *Oh my goodness. I'm the foreigner here. I'm white and I must look out of place. I haven't seen another white face since I landed. Be careful what you say, Emma. Tread carefully and warily.* "Thank you. I'll be on my way." She picked up her suitcase and continued along the track until she came upon a beautiful weatherboard cottage, not at all like a shack as she understood the word. *This must be the place,* she thought, and then noticed a pretty sign edged with painted flowers hanging above a bright green door protected by a sturdy screen door - *The Shack.* She climbed the steps up to the veranda and pulled the cord hanging from an ornate bell.

"Coming!" a shrill voice called and the door opened to reveal a woman in a brightly coloured apron and her hands full of flour. "Hello, young lady. What can I do for you?"

Emma couldn't hide her surprise. "Oh!" she exclaimed wide-eyed. "I expected..."

The woman laughed knowingly. "You expected a black woman," she said, more as a question than a statement.

Emma was embarrassed. "I expected a Jamaican lady," she clarified, hoping her manners would cover her embarrassment.

The woman laughed amicably. "But I am a Jamaican woman," she said. "Born and bred! I'm Dorothy...Dorothy Grant."

"I'm sorry to be so naïve," Emma apologised. "I didn't mean to show my ignorance in that way."

"Don't you worry...what's your name?"

"I'm Emma Williams. I'm escaping the war in Europe and hoping to find a position here at least until the end of the war. Do you have a room for me, please?"

"I do indeed," Dorothy told her. "You are very lucky because some of the Kingston boys who spend their leave here have just returned to their Trinidad base. You chose the right time to arrive, my friend."

"More by luck than good management," Emma said. "It will just be until I find a job, Mrs Grant."

~ * ~

A week later, Emma had gained a live-in position as a housekeeper for an elderly lady whose son was away working for a big sugar company in the United States. The Thomson Estate had been sub-divided and there were several cottages close by, now owned by the local sugar and banana growers. "My previous housekeeper decided to go to work as a cook at the Army base in Trinidad. She said she wanted to do her bit for king and country, but *I know* she was following her young man who is in training there. I tried to talk her out of it, but she wouldn't listen. Her parents didn't object, you see, so who was I to interfere? Good luck to her, I say. I hope all goes well for her."

Emma listened, but didn't comment.

"I'll need you to make my breakfast early each morning," she explained.

"Not a problem, Mrs Thomson," Emma assured her. "I prefer early mornings. Getting up early in this climate is bliss to me. There's no need to stay snuggled up in blankets to keep warm like I often had to do at home."

"Well, I eat breakfast at six o'clock and that means you'll need to be up at five. That's really early, I know, but do you think you can manage that?"

"I certainly can. It sounds wonderful," Emma replied. "I think I am going to enjoy my time with you and I know I shall love living on this beautiful island."

"I love Jamaica, too, I was born and bred here, but a word of warning to you as a stranger...if you go out on your own, stay uptown. Downtown is considered...how should I say it...downtown may not be safe for you, especially at night. Some of the young guys think they can help themselves to other people's property. There's been quite a spate of it recently. I thought with boys going to war, we might guarantee our safety from these young hooligans." She shrugged. "Maybe when the war is over, young people will value life more, their own as well as ours. Who knows what the future will hold?"

"I doubt if I will go out at night, Mrs Thomson," Emma assured her employer. "I'll be happy just to stay home and listen to the radio, maybe read a book occasionally and write letters to my family in England. I have dreamed of a relaxing way of life after living through the London blitz."

"That must have terrible for you. You are obviously a sensible girl. Now, going back to our discussion about your work here, you'll need to organise your time for household chores, make a light lunch for me and then dinner for us both in the evening. I'd like us to get to know each other and how better than over dinner?"

Emma was surprised. "But I'm just your housekeeper, Mrs Thomson. I really shouldn't be sitting at your table and eating with you."

"Why ever not? You will also be my companion when I need company. I shall pay you well for that privilege, mine more than yours, I think."

And so Emma happily settled into a routine that allowed time off in the afternoons when she was able to go to the beach and swim in the cool, blue ocean before returning to make dinner for her employer. Sometimes she would call in to see Dorothy Grant, who offered to teach her to make jerk chicken and oatmeal Jamaican style.

"Mrs Thomson?" Emma ventured to say one morning after she had been doing her new job for a couple of weeks. "Would you like to try some English breakfasts occasionally? I could possibly rustle up a full English as they call it at home."

Mrs Thomson looked over her glasses at the young woman she was growing to like more each day. "I might," she said warily. "I'm not very adventurous when it comes to trying new foods."

Emma laughed. "I wouldn't call English cuisine adventurous, Mrs T. I heard some of the Canadian servicemen calling their NAAFI food bland and uninteresting..."

"Then I don't want it," Mrs Thomson decided on the spot.

"I could spice it up a bit," Emma suggested. "I could make eggs Benedict. That would be considered very posh for any English person. I think we have the ingredients and I'm sure Dorothy would lend me what we don't have. Now *she* seems to have everything in her pantry!"

Mrs Thomson nodded knowingly. "Dorothy Grant takes in a lot of servicemen when they're on leave. I've heard they pay her in food items they smuggle in from the base."

Emma looked wide-eyed at her employer. "Really? Oh, my goodness. Is that legal?"

Mrs Thomson shrugged. "I don't care either way. We are in the middle of a war, and it's every man for himself. I'd rather she were accepting food from them than doing what other landladies do in place of payment. Some of them have been without husbands for months; years even."

Emma, still wide-eyed, gasped. "What *are* you suggesting, Mrs T? Does that really go on? I must be very naïve. I would never even think about that—"

"I'm glad to hear it," Mrs Thomson interrupted. "I wouldn't have employed you if I thought you had loose morals."

Emma suddenly thought about Ann. *I wonder how Ann is. She didn't think she had loose morals. She considered she was doing the soldiers a favour. Well, I guess she was, but she wanted to make them happy before they went to the Front. I guess there's something quite unselfish in that. I think I'll write to her to find out how she's doing. I hope Earl welcomed her with open arms. Goodness knows what she would do if he didn't.*

Mrs Thomson noticed Emma deep in thought. "You are very quiet, dear. Did I say something you didn't agree with?"

Emma felt suddenly awkward. "No, not at all. You just stirred up a memory about one of my shipmates."

"I hope it's a good memory."

"Well, it is and it isn't, Mrs T," Emma said. "I'm not sure I can share it just yet, though. Ann told me a secret and it really isn't mine to tell. I might write to her, though. She gave me a contact address."

Mrs Thomson smiled. "You're a good girl, Emma, and clearly a good friend. Is this young woman living nearby?"

"She went to Spanish Town when she left the ship. Is it far from here?"

"Not very far," Mrs Thomson informed her. "About fourteen miles, half an hour by car. Do you drive?"

Emma shook her head. "I didn't have time to learn before the war started. My dad was posted overseas almost immediately after he was drafted and Mum was never interested."

"I'll teach you," Mrs Thomson said. "I'm too old to drive myself, but I know how. James left his car here when he left. It's a very old Austin, but it still goes. I get old Winston from the plantation down the road to turn over the engine every so often, so what do you say?"

"I don't know what to say," Emma declared. "I can't believe it. Are you sure?"

"I am, and we'll start tomorrow. We can stay on the estate to begin with and then, when you've got the hang of it, you'll be able to use the car and, maybe go to visit your friend."

Emma smiled happily. "Thank you, Mrs T. I don't know what else to say. Thank you so much."

~ * ~

After half a dozen lessons from Mrs Thomson, Emma was ready to go on the road. The old Austin had been covered in dust and rusting a little on the rear fender, but Emma cleaned and polished it as best she could and the little green automobile spluttered its way along, improving with every mile. She took Mrs T. out for drives along the coast and each Thursday, they went to the local store to see if they might subsidise the pantry, food shortages considered, with anything they were unable to provide for themselves on the homestead.

"This is fun, Mrs T..."

"Emma," Mrs Thomson said as they were returning to the house after a short drive into uptown Kingston. "Do you think you might call me by my name? I am Merlene Eugenia Thomson, but Merlene will do; Merle if you are so inclined." Her thoughts were of her growing fondness for the young lady who had suddenly appeared at her door when she most needed somebody to share her life, such that it was. *She's the daughter I never had chance to love and to cherish. God works in mysterious ways. He took my tiny girl, Imogen, into his care before I had time to bond with her and now, almost thirty years later, He has sent this lovely young woman to be with me in my twilight years. Amen to that.*

"But you're my employer, Mrs T. It wouldn't be polite for me to be too familiar."

"But I'm also your friend and I would be delighted if you might call me Merlene."

Emma hesitated, smiled and replied, "All right, Mrs...Merlene, but you'll have to forgive me if I slip up occasionally."

Seven

Several weeks went by and Emma practised her driving each day until she felt confident enough to go on the road without Merlene. One Saturday in October, she decided it was time to try to find Ann and she asked Merlene's permission to use the car. "I would just like to see if Ann is coping in her new life. I hope she has been as lucky as I have. I won't be away too long."

"Stay as long as you like," Merlene encouraged. "I'm sure a short visit won't give you time to catch up properly. Just keep an eye on the weather, though. Actually, there have been no hurricane warnings since the last one at the beginning of June this year. We had everything battened down and then she changed course and left us alone for once. We Jamaicans are always aware that the weather changes sometimes without warning."

"I know," Emma gasped. "We got some sort of warning on the ship and the sea was quite rough for a time, but same as you, we were told the hurricane had changed course. I was so relieved; I can tell you. I wasn't sure my stomach would stand being tossed around in a hurricane." She laughed. "It took me a while to adjust to the rolling of that little ship, but I did it, and I'm quite proud of myself."

"Good for you, Emma," Merlene said. "I just want you to be aware of tropical storms, that's all. And don't be wandering around Spanish Town. We never know what is happening on the streets there. It's a sorry state of affairs when we have to be more than aware that whoever is walking past us just might be after our purses. I'm not trying to frighten you, but have your wits about you and please don't drive if the weather changes for the worse."

"I won't," Emma assured her. "I tried to find a telephone number for Earl Brown, but it seems the name Brown is like the name Smith in England. There are too many to check and, apart from that, I couldn't find any Browns with the address I've been given. I might be going on a wild goose chase. What a coincidence they are combining what must be two of the most common names in the world." She and Merle laughed light-heartedly.

"Well, not everybody has a phone, you know," Merle told her. "I have one because my husband had to be in constant touch with the authorities. Most Jamaicans can't afford a phone and the one or two public telephone boxes they do have seem to be used night and day for couples canoodling, I've been told." She laughed. "What is the world coming to? But if you can't find your friend, you'll just have to come back home." She paused a moment to collect her thoughts. "You could always call in at the Army Recruitment Office. They might have records of the soldiers who returned... Oh dear, I think I have put two and two together and made five."

Emma was puzzled and it showed.

"I decided that if a young woman had a name and address over here, she must have met one of our soldiers when he was serving overseas. Sorry if that comes over as prying."

"Don't be sorry, Merle," Emma replied. "That's part of the story, but I'll tell you the rest when I find Ann and she tells me she's all right."

~ * ~

Emma drove slowly along the street looking for number twenty-seven. She was heeding Merle's words of advice about not wandering around in a place you don't know, and they played on her mind. She locked herself in the car as a precaution. Strangely, there was a piece of derelict land between numbers twenty-five and twenty-nine. She sighed and her thoughts were confused. *So, if there isn't a number twenty-seven, did Earl give Ann a false address? Oh my good lord, I hope not! Poor Ann.* She drove to the end of the street and turned around to drive up the opposite side, just to confirm the house numbers hadn't been mixed up for some reason. She eyed the numbers carefully. *Eighteen, twenty, twenty-two, twenty-four, twenty-six. Oh dear. No twenty-seven.* All the little weatherboard houses were really nothing more than wooden shacks, each with a ramshackle veranda bearing a washing boiler apparently powered by wood burning on a metal tray underneath. *I guess it beats heating the water up first before emptying it into the washtub and pounding the dirty clothes with a posser to make them clean,* Emma thought as she peered hopefully at the last few houses in the street.

Finally, she decided to stop and find somebody, anybody, who might tell her what had happened to the missing house. Getting out of the car and carefully locking the doors again, she walked up the grass verge and tentatively knocked on the door of number twenty-six, which was opposite the space that ought to be number twenty-seven. A large lady opened the door and a look of horror spread across her face. "What you want, girl? We don't want any more white girls coming on our street," she said and began to close the door again.

"What do you mean?" Emma asked. "I'm looking for my friend, Ann Smith. Have you seen her? Do you know where she is?"

The woman looked warily at the distraught Emma. "Look, chile. You seem like a regular girl, but since the other girl came, Earl Brown had no luck at all. She brought demons with her, that one. She not been here more than a few weeks when the house burn down. What are we black folk to think? We never had no trouble here before and it's been quiet since she and Earl left. He got guts, that young guy. Good luck to him. He'll need it."

Emma could not hide her shock and she grabbed hold of the rail to steady herself. "Ann is my friend, and she hasn't a bad bone in her body. You must be mistaken."

The woman folded her arms across her ample bosom and took a stance which indicated she would not be crossed without a fight. "I'm telling you, missy, there be no trouble till she come. People like her get what they deserve."

"You must be talking about a different person," Emma suggested. "The Ann Smith I know has a heart of gold and wouldn't deliberately hurt anybody."

"She hurt my girl right enough, she did. My Adeline was waiting for Earl to come home from the war so's she could aks him to marry her. He didn't want a bar of it. Said he met some white girl in England and then she turn up out of the blue..."

"But you can't make Earl love your daughter if he loved Ann. That doesn't make Ann a bad person."

The woman stood her ground. "Well, if she ain't bad, then how come the house burn down? You tell me that."

Emma looked sadly at the woman. "I really don't want to discuss Ann with you," she said firmly. "I mean no disrespect, but it's clear you don't know her at all. Have you any idea where she and Earl have gone? I really do need to find her, especially now."

"No, I have not," the woman answered. "But if you find them, let me know. I have a bone to pick with Earl Brown and that devil in disguise he has with him."

Emma, so shocked at what she had heard, returned to the car and wondered what to do next.

~ * ~

"I'm not sure I'm at liberty to give you that information, Miss," the kindly army officer said.

"But I'm Ann's friend," Emma pleaded. "She and Mr Brown will vouch for me, I'm sure. If you like, I can obtain a reference from my employer to say I'm a reliable and trustworthy person..."

"I'm sure you are, but rules are rules, and the authorities say I cannot give out information regarding the whereabouts of soldiers who have returned from active service overseas." He looked at the desolation in Emma eyes, cleared his throat as though he were about to deliver an oratory and then whispered, "You might try the lodging house at ninety-four Westland Street…"

Just then, a senior officer, with more pips on his shoulders than Emma could count walked in and the informant stood to attention and saluted. "Everything all right here, Sergeant?"

"All good, sir. I was just telling this young lady that we cannot give out information of returning soldiers." He looked pointedly at Emma.

"Quite right, Sergeant. We would never do that. People cannot just walk in here and demand answers. There's a war on, you know." The senior officer haughtily huffed and puffed and returned to his office.

Emma stood and looked wide-eyed at her man in shining armour. She winked at him and made for the door. "Okay then, Sergeant, I understand," she said loudly. "I'll just have to hope they contact me in the meantime. Thank you, anyway."

~ * ~

The clouds were gathering as Emma drove to Westland Street and there was a stiff breeze blowing in from the ocean. She was mindful of Merle's warning before she left, but the urgency to find Ann blotted out thoughts that she might be putting herself in danger. *Look at that sky,* she told herself, *but I have to see if Ann is with Earl in the lodging house. I can't go home until I have put my mind at ease. Home? That just came into my head. Home is London and yet I feel so comfortable calling Merle's Thomson estate my home. Maybe that's divine intervention.* She smiled to herself. *I knew I would find my niche somewhere in this troubled world.*

She pulled up at the entrance of number ninety-four Westland Street. It was a narrow, blackened brick building three storeys high and the windows looked as if they hadn't been cleaned for months. She looked up and down to see if there was any sign of life and suddenly, as the sun broke through a break in the gathering storm clouds, one window shone brightly amongst the rest. *I can hazard a guess that's Ann's window on the third floor. She'd definitely clean her windows. Her work-space in the galley was always spotlessly clean,* she thought happily. *I've found her.* She looked up to the heavens. *Thank you, Lord.*

Emma found there were two apartments on each floor and she climbed three flights of stairs to the top. She ascertained that Ann and Earl's apartment must be at the front of the building and, when she reached the door, her heart was beating wildly in her chest, not just from her strenuous climb, but also because she could hardly contain her excitement. The door was a dull green colour, but the polished brass number 3A, incongruously shone brightly in the gloom. Emma stared at it for a few seconds before she knocked.

A man's voice called out. "Coming! Just a sec." When the door opened, a young man, balancing on crutches greeted her with a huge welcoming smile. "Hi there," he said. "What can I do for you?"

Emma was struck dumb for a moment, but when she opened her mouth to speak, her voice sounded squeaky and immature. "Oh, er, er...does Ann live here?"

The guy turned away from her and called into the apartment. "Somebody looking for Ann. Is she available?" He shrugged towards Emma.

"Ask who it is," the unmistakable Cockney voice of Ann called out.

"Ann! It's me, Emma!"

There were sounds of shuffling papers and plumping of pillows before Ann replied. "Well, I'll go to the foot of our stairs," she shrilled. "Ask her in, Earl, for goodness sake. I can't come while I'm feeding the baby. Oh my lord, am I glad to see you, Ems. I have missed you so much." Her voice trembled, and she sobbed unashamedly.

Earl stood aside and gestured to Emma to follow the passage to the living room. She stood, framed in the doorway, and lovingly took in the sight of Ann discreetly nursing a tiny brown child with a mop of tight black curls on its little head. Both women allowed happy tears to course down their cheeks, and Emma went to sit by her friend as she finished her motherly task.

When she had recovered her composure, Emma told Ann, "It is so good to see you."

"I have so much to tell you," Ann beamed, "not least to introduce you to Earl."

Earl nodded in Emma's direction. "Nice to meet you, Emma. I have heard so much about you. It's good to put a face to the name now." His voice was soft and gentle, exactly how Ann had described him to Emma when they were on the ship.

"Likewise," Emma replied, "and who is this little one?"

Ann grinned. "This is Gloria Marie Brown, Glory for short," Ann said as she handed the baby to Emma and did up her blouse. "Can you burp her for me while I make myself decent?"

Emma looked wary. "What do I do?" she asked nervously. "I have never held a baby; in fact, I have only seen them in prams on the Fulham Road."

"Just put her over your shoulder and pat her back. With a bit of luck, she'll burp straight away. She usually does," and then to Earl, "Just help Emma get the baby in the right position, will you, honey? She looks absolutely scared to death." Ann laughed heartily and, as soon as Earl placed the baby over Emma's shoulder, Gloria burped loudly and spat milk down the back of Emma's dress.

"Good one, little girl. That's a great way to introduce yourself to Auntie Em. Welcome to the realms of motherhood, Emma."

Earl hobbled into the kitchen to find a damp cloth to wipe away the posset from Emma's dress. "Sorry, Miss Emma," he said shyly. "I hope you will still love our little girl. She doesn't know yet what she should and shouldn't do." He grinned and winked. "We'll certainly make sure she knows not to throw up on visitors in future."

"Not a problem," Emma replied. "I was just surprised that it came so quickly." She handed the baby back to Ann who went to place her in the crib by the side of the sofa.

"I'll just make you a cuppa, and we'll have a piece of the banana bread I made this morning, and then we'll have a chat," Ann told her. "Earl won't mind if he has to listen to two girls nattering on. There is so much to tell."

"I intended to write to you, but I never got around to it," Emma admitted.

"It's p'raps as well you didn't," Ann said casually. "The house ain't there anymore. I'll tell you about that in a sec."

"I already know some of it, I think," Emma disclosed. "I spoke to a woman on the opposite side of Jackson Street—"

"Oh no," Earl groaned. "Please don't tell me it was Albertina..."

"I didn't ask her name, but she was very rude and obstreperous—"

"That's Albertina," Ann joined in. "She wouldn't have anything good to say about me. She bombarded me with insults as soon as I arrived."

Emma took her friend's hand as she listened to the story. She heard first how Earl had inherited his mother's house when she passed away. She had been a single mother and had worked herself into her grave to give her son a good home and a good education.

"It wasn't easy for her," Earl explained, "but she made sure I had the upbringing she wanted...a comfortable home, always food on the table and always clean clothes, even if they were hand-me-downs and repaired until they couldn't hold one more stitch." He smiled at the thought. "We were poor but happy."

Ann continued. "When I arrived, Earl had only recently been allowed home after his rehabilitation. He couldn't go back in the army because of his injuries...he lost a foot." She added the last bit quietly. "To me he's perfect," she said lovingly in Earl's direction, and he smiled adoringly back at her. "Albertina's daughter, Adeline, was sitting with Earl when I arrived at his door. If you'd seen us, Em! We both burst into tears and held each other as though we would never let go. Adeline was livid and didn't hold back. She screamed at me to leave them alone and asked what a white girl would be doing here to take her fiancé off her. Earl was as dumbstruck as I was. He'd never asked her to marry him and was never really a close friend, but she'd taken it upon herself to look after him when he was released from hospital, so I guess she ain't all bad."

Emma nodded knowingly. "Albertina told me that her daughter was asking him to marry her just as you arrived. She said you had brought shame to the street, and there was no room for a white girl to be in their community. She figured the house had burned down because of some evil spell you had cast. Fortunately, she doesn't know where you are. If she sees Earl again, she says she has a bone to pick with him."

Earl shrugged. "And I'm supposed to be afraid of that? I can't prove it, but I'm as sure as I can be that Adeline got her brother to set my house alight when we were out. The police said it looked like I had gone out and left the fire unguarded, but I always make sure the fireguard is round the boiler before I go out. We only light a fire when we need hot water, and Ann wanted to set about washing curtains and bedlinen before she had the baby."

"We were only out half an hour," Ann added. "We came back to find the fire brigade—such that it is—trying desperately to put the fire out."

Emma was shocked. "Oh, my goodness," she wailed. "How terrible! Did you manage to save anything at all?"

"Nothing. Our houses are mostly made of wood, not like yours in London. What you see here is what my army mates have contributed, but I'm going to sell the block where the house stood and then I'll build somewhere well away from here. I don't want my wife and my child living in squalor, and these lodging houses aren't where I would choose to live. I want better for my family."

Emma looked wide-eyed at both Ann and Earl. "Wife?"

Ann nodded. "We got a special licence as soon as I arrived and just had a private wedding with a couple of witnesses from the celebrant's office. We didn't want to live over the brush. I wish you could have been there, Em. You could have been my bridesmaid."

"I would have loved that," Emma responded, and she went on to tell them of her good fortune in meeting Merle and all that it involved. "She's my second mother. I am so fond of her. I wouldn't be here with you now, but for her teaching me to drive and lending me her son's old car." She looked at the clock on the dresser. "Oh, it's four o'clock already. I must be on my way, and I've been warned to watch the weather for storm clouds gathering. It looked a bit dark when I arrived, but I hope they've blown over. Now I know where you are, I'll come and see you again, if that's okay with you."

"Are you kidding?" Ann said. "I'd be sad if you didn't."

"And I'll ask Merle if I can ask you over to our place for lunch, or tea, or whatever. I'm sure she'll be fine with that. Thanks for the tea. I'm so happy I found you."

Emma sang to herself all the way back. *She gave her heart to a soldier boy and he now plays a hero's part. If you can't take his place in the uniform, then you can't take his place in her heart...* She'd first heard the song at the Hammersmith Palais and then Roy Rogers could be heard frequently on the radio. Merle's radio was old and crackly, but it had provided Emma with a lot of entertainment. She and Merle had been to the movie theatre, such that it was. It was literally a shed with a projector and a large screen. Roy Rogers' movies were always showing, or so it seemed. They'd already seen *King of the Cowboys* and *The Man from Music Mountain* and that week, there was another one advertised, *Silver Spurs*. She smiled to herself. *I think Roy Rogers' movies are the only ones available just now. I'm not sure if real cowboys sing while they round up cattle, but I don't mind seeing Roy Rogers. He sure is handsome.* She laughed out loud. *Look at me! I'm going all goo-goo eyed over a movie star. I guess it's seeing Ann and Earl so much in love that's made me feel the warmth of romance. Maybe my time to find a nice guy will come...someday...*

Just as she pulled up on the drive of the Thomson Estate, Emma was startled when a loud crash of thunder and a flash of lightning lit up the evening sky and torrential rain came seemingly out of nowhere. She grabbed a magazine from the passenger seat and covered her head as she ran from the garage to the house. "Phew," she gasped as she closed the door behind her. "Good timing or what?"

"Just in time," Merle agreed. "Come on into the kitchen and we'll make dinner together. A mixture of Jamaican and British cuisine, and we'll see what sort of a concoction we can come up with." She busied herself with arranging spices for the chicken she was offering as her contribution and Emma found all manner of vegetables to roast— sweet potatoes, carrots and eggplant, together with one of the tins of butter beans that Dorothy Grant had off-loaded after her soldiers had been over on leave.

"This is a feast fit for a king," Merle said as they tucked into their joint effort. "I don't cook very often as you know, Emma, but it does me good to keep my hand in."

"Wait and see what I've got for dessert," Emma told her before she produced the banana bread Ann had pushed into her hand as she left. "It's been a good day, in spite of the heavens opening just as I arrived back."

"You're a good girl, Emma," Merle told her. "I'm so glad you found me."

"My pleasure on all counts," Emma said. "No contest!"

Eight

Four years passed. Emma's life was happy and she felt so at home in uptown Kingston. Her letters home were full of happiness and pleasurable things and those she received in return were increasingly full of doom and gloom. It was in late nineteen forty-five that her father had been returned from a prison camp where he had almost starved to death and, apparently, according to Aunt Edith, *'he just sits in his wheelchair all day and says very little. In the three years he has been home, he's grown old and disinterested in everything...He never asks about your mum, or of you, and I worry that he doesn't even know who I am...'*

Emma had replied often and asked if her aunt thought she should return to Windsor, but her father's doctors had implied that it wasn't absolutely necessary for her to return at that time since his therapist had indicated he was unlikely ever to go back to be the man he used to be. Aunt Edith had said he never asked where Emma was and her letters to Emma became less frequent, but she did say... *'I tend to agree with the doctors, Emma. Too many things for him to take in might be too much for him. You seem to have a good life over there, and there would be very little for you here just at the moment. Life is hard for everybody, so stay there as long as you like, but don't forget us, will you? I can't believe I'm saying that to you, considering how much I tried to stop you from going in the first place. You'll know in your heart when you want to come home. I firmly believe that.*

Emma discussed her misgivings with Merle, who offered to give her the money to buy a ticket home if she felt it necessary to look after her family in England.

"Thank you, Merle, but I don't need to go just now. Auntie Edith has given me her blessing to stay. I think she just wants what is best for me and, according to her, there's not a lot happening in England at the moment. My dad is apparently in a fragile state and seeing me might just tip him over the edge. It's sad, but I'm here for the time being." She paused momentarily. "I'll *have* to go back some time, I understand that, but I'll know when the time is right."

~ * ~

Several months later, Emma was having dinner with Merle as usual when Merle asked casually, "Remember when you posted the letter I had written to James?"

"I do, but that was months ago and I thought he had replied."

Merle put her finger to her lips to ask Emma to be quiet. "I need to talk with you about something quite serious." She spoke almost in a whisper. "He did reply, and he gave me the go-ahead to do what I wanted. He has no interest in coming back here, and he agreed for me to leave this house and all it contains to you..."

Emma was dumbfounded. "You can't do that!" she exclaimed.

"I can, and I have. My will bequeaths it to you to do as you like with it. James will have all the monetary assets and the land will be sold off to the highest bidder, that is, apart from the generous garden around the house."

Emma began to cry. "Oh Merle, I don't know what to say. We'll be here together for ages yet. I know you haven't been feeling well for a while, but—"

"Please don't cry, Emma. I love you as a daughter and James really hasn't had time for me since he moved to New York. When he married, he told me more than once that I wasn't his priority. His wife and his children must come first and to a point, I agree with him, but sometimes I wish I could feel the love he gave me as he was growing up. We were so close. To pacify myself, I often repeat the old adage…*a daughter's a daughter all her life, but a son is a son 'til he marries a wife*. That's very true and I have learned to live with it."

"That sounds very sad," Emma told her. "I'm sure he still loves you deep down."

"Maybe, but he doesn't often show it." She paused poignantly. "He doesn't seem to want to make the effort to come home, even occasionally. Still, when he replied to my letter that outlined the contents of my will, he said he was more than happy with it and agreed to let you have the house. He totally understood why I wanted to do that for you. I think he appreciates your being here, although he would never admit it. You've taken over his responsibilities, you see."

Emma was at a loss what to say. "Oh Merle, I came here of my own free will and I have been so lucky to have found my job with you. I hope James doesn't think I set out to wheedle my way into your affections."

"Not at all," Merle told her firmly. "James understands all too well that, but for you, he would be burdened with the responsibility of his aging mother. I know him well enough and he would definitely have made his feelings known if he were unhappy with the situation as it is now. I wish I could say he was his father's son, but I can't." She paused and looked to the heavens as if for inspiration.

Emma remained silent.

"No, my dear, we are all happy with my decision…truly. You are the daughter I always wanted and I love you as such."

"And you have been a wonderful replacement for the mother I lost in the Blitz. I am so happy with you. Thank you for being…well, for being you."

As if that conversation had been an omen, it was only a couple of weeks later that Merle's health began to deteriorate and she noticeably looked much older and more frail. Emma found herself becoming her nurse as well as her housekeeper.

"I'm a burden to you, aren't I?" Merle said quietly one morning as Emma gave her breakfast in bed as had become the norm during the past few weeks.

"Not at all," Emma chastised. "I'm happy to care for you. You have been like a mother to me the last few years and I wouldn't dream of allowing anybody else to look after you. I'll get you well and then we can start going out again."

"But you...going out...enjoy yourself...keep you here," Merle protested, her voice feeble and broken, but there was no mistaking the sadness in her tone. "Your friends..." She seemed to be gasping at every word.

"Merle," Emma said tenderly. "I'm happy to be here. The time I have been with you has been wonderful and I wouldn't change a thing. My single friends all have their own responsibilities in different ways. The guys at the bowling club have jobs to hold down and a couple of them are looking to get married next year. You've met my best friends, Ann and Earl, on numerous occasions and, with Earl forming his own car mechanics company just down the road from here, and Ann looking after Gloria and little Edward, she is happy to be a stay-at- home mum."

Merle smiled weakly and Emma noticed how much she was finding it difficult to communicate. "L-l-lovely family," Merle offered and then, making a bold effort to be clear and distinct, "James should be here; too many things in New York; sugar industry; big changes; can't leave his family...come home...look after me." Her voice was low, yet it had the distinctive tone of disappointment, and Emma noticed Merle's eyes were full of sadness and unshed tears.

Emma leaned forward in order to hear more clearly what was being said.

Merle took Emma's hand and squeezed it gently, affectionately. She lay back on her pillows and closed her eyes. She smiled, took in a long, deep breath, and exhaled very slowly. That was the last time Merlene breathed, and Emma sank to her knees and wept uncontrollably.

~ * ~

"I've sorted out everything with the lawyer," James said after the funeral. "There'll be no need for me to come back here. You'll be just fine here on your own?" The question sounded more like a statement, an assumed *fait accompli* on James's part.

"I'll be fine, but are you sure about leaving Jamaica?" she asked, trying to keep her tone light and friendly. "You appear to be quite happy with the situation regarding the house, but I think your mother would have liked you and your family to stay a little while... you know, like old times. She often said that the children would love it here. I can make up the beds in the guest rooms if you like. It seems an unnecessary expense for you to stay in the hotel."

James raised his eyebrows and looked Emma in the eye. "My mother is dead. How would she know if the children were enjoying themselves or not? No, I have to be back in New York as soon as possible for work, and the children can't be out of school for too long. This is your home now, not ours. We love New York and it's where we want to be. I left Jamaica behind a long time ago."

Emma remained silent but shrugged resignedly.

"By the way, Miss Williams..."

"Emma, please..."

"By the way, *Miss Williams*, the old jalopy is yours, too, if you want it. I'm surprised it's still going..."

"Your mother made sure it was kept in good running order by having it serviced regularly, especially since my friend's husband came home from the war and opened his own workshop. Thank you very much, *Mr Thomson*. It will be useful to me in more ways than I can count," Emma said more tersely than she would have liked to convey, but her thoughts were less than charitable. *What a supercilious man! I am so determined not to let him see my contempt. He is so cold, so unfeeling, and so insensitive. Even his wife and children cower in the background. I'm glad Merle isn't here to see it for herself. What a complicated character he is. His generosity is clear and very much appreciated, but he does everything with such bad grace.*

"Are you sure everything is in order here?" she asked politely. "You have my word that I will look after the place. I'll keep you informed if my plans change."

"No need," James replied. "When I leave, I shall be glad to have it out of my hands. Best thing I ever did to leave all this behind. Ah, here's our cab. Goodbye, Miss Williams. My lawyer will let you know when the land is sold." He offered his hand and Emma took it limply, deliberately not offering a firm, confident handshake.

"Goodbye, Mr Thomson," she said and walked into the house without waving as they drove off.

~ * ~

Emma asked Ann if she might have time to help with sorting out Merle's things. "I don't know where to start," she said. "I feel like I am intruding on her privacy."

Ann smiled at her friend. "I know what you mean," she said gently, "but it has to be done. All this is yours and, until you clear out Merle's belongings, it won't feel like your home. You need to put your own stamp on it. You are so lucky, Em. Who'd o' thought it? Emma Williams, property owner!" She nudged Emma playfully and they laughed together, sighing and gasping in awe as they went over what had happened since they met on that ship almost five years ago.

"I'll be off now," Ann said after they had made great progress in boxing up Merle's belongings, most of which would go to the local church for distribution to those who were doing it tough after the war. "I'll see you later. Call me if you need me again."

Later that evening, Emma sat on her sofa and looked across the room at the boxes of Merle's possessions she and Ann had packed away. She had seen a new charity shop had opened up in Kingston, and she decided Merle would have wanted her things to go somewhere they might be used again, so she would load up the car and take the boxes there tomorrow. Emma's thoughts were confused. *Merle would like that,* she reassured herself. *Dear, dear Merle. How kind and caring she was. How on earth could she have borne an arrogant son like James?* She stood and shook her head to clear the ungracious thoughts of him from her mind, then ...*Don't think such things. At least James has made sure he dealt with everything he needed to before he left. I doubt if I shall ever meet him again.* She inhaled deeply. *I think never would be too soon.* She walked into the kitchen to make a cup of tea and, seeing a small box on the kitchen table, she remembered she needed to go through Merle's paperwork before she burned what was way out of date. Burning it was the only way, for privacy and security reasons.

The old bills and bank statements were easy to discard and burn without so much as a glance. Two envelopes stood out from the rest. One was tied with a pink ribbon and the other, blue. Emma held them in her hands for a while before she gained the confidence to open them. *I recall Merle telling me she lost a little girl. Maybe this envelope contains her birth certificate,* she thought as she opened it. It was indeed a birth certificate and a death certificate. *How sad.* She sniffed, conscious of the fact that Merle's death was still very raw in her mind, and she wiped away the tears again, tears that made her remember the night she lost her mother, unable to save her from the nightmare that was happening in London at that time.

Sunday, 12 July 1903. Father: Gordon James Thomson; Mother: Merlene Eugenia Thomson, née Clarke; Occupation of father: Plantation owner; Child – female: Imogen Elizabeth. Then she read the death certificate as again, tears trickled down her cheeks: *Age of child: 3 weeks; Cause of death: Heart defect.*

"Oh, my goodness," Emma cried. "Poor Merle. She only had three weeks with her little girl. How do you recover from something like that?" She stopped abruptly. *You are talking to yourself, Emma,* but she returned the documents to the envelope and neatly tied the pink ribbon in a pretty bow as she had found it.

The envelope with the blue ribbon was bigger and thicker than the one that contained baby Imogen's papers. Emma's mind was in overdrive. *Please Lord, don't say Merle suffered multiple infant deaths while trying to make her little family. I can't bear it. Maybe I shouldn't pry, but I need to know what I'm discarding.*

She pondered a while longer as she fingered the package, needing to be sure in her own mind that she wasn't being too inquisitive. *It must be about boy babies, seeing the ribbon is blue. How organised was Merle?* Emma smiled to herself. *I guess I'd be the same. There must be a name for people who are obsessed with having everything in order. It's like a demanding compulsion sometimes.* Slowly she pulled on the end of the ribbon, untied the bow and slid her fingers inside the envelope. She paused while she overcame the feelings of prying again. Taking in a deep breath, she removed the documents from the envelope.

The Process of Adoption, she read, and then there was a very official looking form filled out in typed print, not hand-written. *Applicant/s: Gordon James Thomson and Merlene Eugenia Thomson. Reason for application: Inability to complete pregnancy. Six miscarriages.* "Oh, my lord," Emma whispered. "How sad." She continued reading and after several questions pertaining to income and suitability of applicants and of accommodation ready to house a child...*Child available: Boy at birth. Birth mother agrees to immediate adoption. Name of child: To be decided by adoptive parents.*

Emma sighed. *I'll have to send these to James and I'll ask him if he would like the documents relating to his sister.*

She called James later that day. "I have found some personal documents regarding you and your sister. Would you like me to send them to you?"

There was what seemed like a long pause. "Er...er...what sort of documents?" James asked tentatively.

Emma was wary. *Perhaps I ought not to have read them. Oh dear.* "There's a birth and death certificate for Imogen and then a pile of papers pertaining to your ... your—"

"My what?" James spat. "Come on girl, spit it out."

"Well, I'm not sure if I ought to have read them, but I was trying to sort out Merle's stuff and these were in a box with old invoices and paid bills. I'm sorry if it looks like I was prying..."

"If you're talking about my adoption papers, well no, I don't want them..."

"But your birth certificate is amongst them," Emma explained. "I thought perhaps you might wish to trace your heritage sometime."

"You do too much thinking, Miss Williams," James told her. "Send them if you must. You have the address?"

"I do," Emma said tersely. *I have your dear mother's address book, but you wouldn't want to know that, would you? Too mundane for your hectic life.* "What about Imogen's documents?"

"I don't want those," he said equally tersely. "Destroy them. They're no use to anybody. I'll look out for my papers in the mail. Thank you, Miss Williams. Goodbye."

Emma replaced the receiver and flopped onto the sofa in the drawing room. *What a selfish, arrogant, pompous bastard he is,* she silently confirmed for herself again. *Sorry Lord, for my uncouth thoughts and condemning choice of words, but that man would make a parson swear. There is no way I'll destroy baby Imogen's papers. I'll keep them as a testament to Merle. I know she would like that. I understand now why Merle couldn't say he was his father's son. I'm as sure as I can be that Gordon Thomson was the perfect gentleman and Merle couldn't attribute James's traits to those of his adoptive father. Maybe he is his biological father's son. What sort of a guy would leave a girl to bring up a child alone and have nothing to do with the child he had fathered?...Hold on, Emma, you are getting carried away with presumptions here and it really is none of your business. How would you know the circumstances of that situation?* Suddenly she thought of Ann and motherhood and sex. *Look at me,* she told herself silently. *Almost twenty-seven years and still a virgin.* She shivered involuntarily and busied herself with completing the task in hand. She parcelled up the documents for James and made sure little Imogen's papers were consigned to her room with her own precious belongings.

Nine

Several months later, Emma had made the house into her home and was relaxing, listening to Merle's nineteen-forties records on the old phonograph she hadn't wanted to throw out with the majority of Merle's other furniture. *Show me the way to go home,* Frank Crumit sang. *I'm tired and I want to...*There was suddenly a loud knocking on her door. Emma looked at the clock on the mantlepiece. *Hmm, eight o'clock. Who could be visiting at this time?* She opened the door tentatively and found Leroy, Earl's assistant mechanic, standing there in his Sunday best and looking very pleased with himself. The two had met a few times previously at Earl's house.

"What are you doing here?" she asked pleasantly.

"I thought you might like to take a walk with me, Miss Emma," Leroy said shyly.

"Did you now?" she said. "And what made you think that?"

"Well, if you'd rather not, I understand," he said. "After all, you are a white lady and I'm a bl—"

"Stop right there, Leroy Morgan," she snapped. "I see people... not black or white, just people, so don't you be suggesting otherwise. I'm saying no to your invitation at this moment in time because it's after dark and I don't think it appropriate to go walking with anybody without prior warning."

"Oh," was all Leroy could say.

"Maybe you and I might meet for coffee at the Café Pearl after church tomorrow," she suggested.

"But you don't go to my church," Leroy said.

"No, I don't, but I will be at the Café Pearl at twelve noon precisely," she told him. "Maybe we can have a bite to eat too. What do you think?"

"I think that's just swell, Miss Emma. Thank you." He grinned endearingly. "Thank you. Miss Emma. I'll be there. See you then." He turned on his heels and seemingly skipped down the driveway like a very happy schoolboy.

Emma shook her head slowly, smiling at the vision of a grown man dancing from her door to the strains of Frank Crumit still asking to be shown the way home.

The following morning, she was up early as usual. She had breakfast, showered and was dressed by nine. *I have time to write home before I go to meet Leroy,* she thought and busied herself with spreading out her writing paper and letters to which she was replying across the table. Picking up and re-reading the latest letter from her aunt, she began to write... *Dear Auntie Edith and Dad* ...She stopped almost as soon as she had started. She sighed deeply, surprised by her thoughts. *Suddenly I am homesick. I want to go home.* She became pensive, sad almost. *I don't understand it at all, although I guess it was inevitable I would feel homesick at some point. I have this lovely home and I love Jamaica so much, but sitting here trying to write this letter fills me with longing to see England again. I want to see Dad, even though he might not know who I am and I want to see Auntie Edith and everybody else I left behind.* She shivered involuntarily, put the top on her pen and tidied up the table. *I'll write properly after I've seen Leroy.* She smiled to herself. *I hope he isn't hoping for anything more than lunch.* She shook her head in an effort to rid her mind of such inappropriate thoughts. *My goodness, Emma Williams. What are you suggesting? You haven't even considered anything more than friendship with any of your friends, white or black,* she silently chastised herself and, as she looked in the mirror to make sure she was presentable, she stuck out her tongue at self-deprecating thoughts she didn't understand herself. *Girl, look at yourself! You aren't ready to settle down just yet...* "Are you?" she asked the girl in the mirror. She shrugged and banished the thoughts from her mind. *Come on, Miss Emma. Let's go and meet Leroy. Lunch and friendly banter is exactly what we need just now.*

Leroy was standing outside the Café Pearl when she arrived. His welcoming smile told Emma she was in for a very pleasant lunch and she smiled too as she waved from a few yards away. "Good morning!" she called as she approached.

Leroy looked at his watch. "Good afternoon," he prompted. "You are nearly two minutes late!" He laughed heartily as he continued, "Just joking. It's good to see you, Miss Emma."

"Leroy," Emma reproached amicably. "Emma will do, please. You don't have to call me Miss Emma."

"Sorry, Miss...That's the way I been raised. My mom always say, *manners makes the man* and I don't want to disrespect a lady."

"That's wonderful," Emma confirmed, "but we are friends, aren't we? Please call me just Emma."

"Okay, Just Emma, I can do that."

Emma nudged him playfully. "Touché, Leroy," she said, laughing at his little joke. "Now we have that settled, let's have some lunch."

~ * ~

Later they sat in her garden drinking lemonade and discussing how their lives had panned out. "I would never have thought in a million years I would be living in Jamaica and owning my own house," Emma mused. "I fled the Blitz on a whim... well, on the say-so of a comparative stranger."

"That was very brave of you," Leroy said. "I must say, I'm glad you did. I wouldn't have met you otherwise."

Emma was taken aback. "You wouldn't know what you'd missed, though, would you?" she replied laughing.

"No, that's true, Emma, but when Earl told me Ann had a lovely English friend, I was keen to meet you. Earl is so happy with his English wife." He looked down at his glass of lemonade and waited for Emma's reply.

Emma was shocked. Her thoughts were in overdrive. *Oh, my dear lord. How did our conversation get to this point? What do I say? He looks so nervous, and I'm being very presumptuous.* "They are," she offered, "and they met in such extreme circumstances. I can't imagine—"

"Can't imagine what, Emma?" Leroy dared to ask. "Being married to a black guy?"

"What are you talking about, Leroy?" she snapped. "That's the second time you have brought my attention to the colour of your skin. What is the matter with you?"

Leroy shifted in his seat. "I've never met a white girl who hasn't turned away at the mere sight of me," he mumbled, "until I met you."

Emma felt her hackles rise. "Look," she said firmly. "I have told you more than once, I see a person, not the colour of his skin. You might not like what I'm going to say, but I'll say it anyway. You seem to have a massive chip on your shoulder, Leroy. Be proud of who you are. Don't belittle yourself. You are a wonderful young man, a man who works hard and who has all the qualities of being a good husband and father. You will make some girl happy one day—"

"Are you giving me the brush off before I've even asked you to go steady?" Leroy ventured.

Emma looked him straight in the eye. "Maybe I am," she said gently. "I'm not looking to fall in love at the moment, and marriage isn't on my agenda, but I like you and I still want to be your friend."

Leroy looked crestfallen, threw his arms up in the air dramatically and then roared with laughter. "Well, that tells *me* then, doesn't it?" he said. "Don't worry, Emma. I guess I'll have to go and find a nice black girl and, before you tell me about that big log I am carrying on my shoulder, you are right. Having a black wife would solve all my problems."

"That's a terrible thing to say, Leroy Morgan," Emma scolded. "I didn't want to make you feel bad." She looked at him and smiled. "We're still friends, aren't we?"

"Of course! You are just what I need, a friend who tells it the way it is. I did think at one point I might be more than a friend, but it seems my timing stinks, doesn't it, you not wanting to fall in love an' all?"

"Well, yes it does," Emma agreed. "Strange though it may seem, this morning, right out of the blue, I was feeling very homesick and I think I might just go back home for a while. There are things I need to catch up on and people whom I need to see. It's been a while..." She covered her face with her hands to try to hide the tears.

Leroy went up to her and held her close. "Don't cry, sweet Emma. Let me give you a Leroy hug to make you feel better."

Accepting the warm, friendly hug he had given her, Emma held him at arms' length and looked into his eyes. "Another time, another place, Leroy, we might have taken this further, but not just now. Be happy, dear friend."

Leroy hugged her close again. "You too, Em."

Admitting she was happy with her single status made Emma assess her life. Her mind was full of thoughts that thus far had been alien to her. *Why now?* she asked herself as she watched Leroy walk down her driveway. He turned and waved as he arrived where the drive met the road and she waved back before she returned to the letter writing she had left. *Surely it can't be the fact that Leroy had intentions to ask me to go steady. I like him, but not in that way.* She took up her pen again and returned to the letter she had almost started previously to her aunt and her dad. *Dear Auntie Edith and Dad, I'm coming home. Not sure when, but I am going to start making plans soon...*

Ten

London - June 1948.

"Come on, man. Stop daydreaming and get to the bottom of this ramp."

BJ turned to find a white girl smiling at him. "Sorry, ma'am. I didn't mean to delay you."

The girl shook her head slowly and still smiling, she nudged him forward again. "I'd like to put my feet on home ground as soon as possible. I've been away far too long. Please..."

BJ quickened his pace as much as the throngs of people ahead of him would allow. He turned to face the girl again and shrugged apologetically. "You'll have to tell them," he said, indicating that his fellow passengers didn't seem to understand the need to go faster.

Suddenly, the girl lurched forward forcing BJ to catch her in order to avoid being floored by a very large, brutish man pushing recklessly through. "Watch out, man!" BJ called, but the guy left them *standing in his wake with looks of dismay on their faces. He grinned at the girl, a sparkling white beaming smile. "That's the way to do it," he said as he looked into the eyes of the girl who had unexpectedly fallen into his arms. Feeling suddenly awkward, he eased her away gently, making sure she was on solid ground. Somehow, after only a few seconds, they found themselves stepping off the gangplank onto the jetty.*

"Thank you," the girl said.

"Emma! Over here!" were loud cries coming from the right, a short distance away.

Without so much as a smile, she was gone, running into the arms of her waiting family.

~ * ~

The first couple of weeks were spent settling in again at her aunt's Windsor home. Her room was just as she had left it. "I thought Dad would be in my room," she told her aunt as she unpacked the day she arrived back.

"I had to make the dining room his bedroom, for obvious reasons," her aunt replied, and she looked extremely sad.

"Sorry, Auntie Edith. I didn't think. Does he speak at all? He doesn't seem pleased to see me, and I am truly happy to see him. Now I know I wasn't orphaned during the war. I have so much to ask him and tell him. I do so want him to be happy to see me again."

Her aunt smiled weakly. "He grunts occasionally and somehow finds his voice when he wants to pass an antagonistic opinion. I hate to say it, but not much pleases him. He rarely gets out of his wheelchair when the district nurses tell him to try to walk a few steps every day. I'm sure he could have been walking to the park by now if he'd just put his mind to it."

"That's sad," Emma said. "He certainly isn't the dad I saw leaving to go to fight in Italy. He was such a loving husband and dad, and a very proud soldier. He's only forty-eight years old, though, and he looks like an old man. It upsets me to see him like that. I hope I'll be able to talk to him and tell him all about my Jamaican life. Oh, Auntie, it was so good in every way..."

"It sounded like it in your letters," Edith replied. "Who'd have thought you would return home being the owner of a big house in Kingston. I hope it wasn't bought from the proceeds of slave labour—"

"Please don't go down that road, Auntie," Emma interrupted. "I never asked and I was never told. Merle was the kindest, most adorable lady you could ever wish to meet, so I can't imagine her being cruel to anybody..." She stopped as she thought of James, the adopted son. *Well, I could imagine James being bombastic and full of his own importance, but he wasn't around in the days of slavery. Come to think of it, I doubt if Merle was even old enough to be a part of all that. Maybe her grandparents, or great-grandparents... I don't want to think about those times, anyway.* "Maybe one day we can all go and have a holiday in my house," she suggested. "I'm sure you would love it and you could meet all my friends, especially Ann and Earl and their brood."

"Have you left your house all locked up while you're away?" Edith asked.

"No," Emma told her. "I have allowed a friend to stay in it while I'm away. He'll look after it, and he'll no doubt have his new wife with him before I get back there."

"Oh, he's married then?" Edith asked, appearing to be genuinely interested.

"No, not yet," she admitted. "He's looking for a nice bl... Jamaican girl to settle down with and I'm sure he won't be too long before he finds his soulmate."

"It all sounds very desultory to me," Edith commented.

"What do you mean, *desultory?*" Emma asked laughing.

"Lacking purpose, no enthusiasm," her aunt said. "If he's ensconced in a big house, he might be entertaining one lady after another. Are you sure you can trust this person with your house? I mean, from all accounts it's a massive place and so must be worth a lot of money."

"You don't appear to have much trust in anybody, Auntie, me included. I'd trust Leroy with my life, honestly, I would. Don't worry. I have it all under control."

~ * ~

After two weeks adjusting to her life back in England and trying to engage her father in conversation without success, Emma decided she would try to find Mavis, who had been with her at the Hammersmith Palais the night her mother had died in the Blitz. She went to the Red Lion Pub; the hostelry Mavis's parents had kept for a number of years.

"Oh, my good lord," Mrs Taylor exclaimed when Emma appeared at the bar. "How long have you been back?"

Emma grinned. "Just a couple of weeks," she said. "Is Mavis home?"

"Well, yes, she's at home, but not here anymore. She got married and lives in Richmond now…"

"My word!" Emma cried. "That's posh, isn't it? Did she marry a millionaire?"

Mrs Taylor laughed. "No, but her husband has a good job in the city. He's a chef and works at the Ritz."

"Oh my, my!" Emma gushed. "I'm impressed. Does she have a phone? I can call her from my aunt's in Windsor. My auntie has recently had a phone installed. It's a party line, but she is so thrilled with it. We're all getting a bit posh, aren't we?"

"We are," Mrs Taylor agreed. "Who'd o' thought a few years ago we'd all have telephones in our houses? That's progress for yer!"

"A pint o' bitter, please love," a guy said as he reached the bar.

"Okay, darlin'," Mrs Taylor told him. "Go and sit down and I'll bring it over in a tick." And then to Emma, "I'll give you our Maeve's number when I've served this young gentleman. Can't keep the punters waiting." She smiled, took the pint of ale to the client and then produced a slip of paper from under the counter on which she wrote the telephone number for Emma.

"Thanks, Mrs Taylor. I'll phone Mavis soon, but if you see her before I do, don't tell her I'm here. I want to surprise her."

She decided to call Mavis as soon as she arrived back in Windsor.

"What number are you calling?" the operator asked.

"Richmond five-eight-seven," Emma said and waited to be connected.

"Just hold on while I put you through."

"Richmond five-eight-seven," Mavis said. "This is Mavis Martinelli speaking. Who's calling?"

Emma grinned to herself. "Guess who?" she answered.

"Is this a nuisance call? I'll have to report you if..." Mavis asked.

"Only if you don't recognise the voice of the girl you were under the table with at the Hammersmith Palais...and I don't mean with drinking too much..."

"We wouldn't have dared," Mavis responded with happy recognition of the caller's voice. "Emma Williams! When did you get back?"

"A couple of weeks ago. Can we meet up? We have so much catching up to do. For one thing, I want to know how you hooked up with a chef and an Italian one, by the sound of your name."

Mavis giggled like a schoolgirl. "I know," she said. "And I'm over the moon about it. I'm up the duff, Em, but we can still meet up. It won't be at the Palais though. I don't think anybody would ask an eight months pregnant woman to dance." She laughed again. "How about you? Are you married yet?"

Emma breathed in deeply. *Oh Maeve, don't ask that. It really irritates me. Why do people have to question my status?* she silently asked herself. "No, not yet. I haven't met Mr Right, but maybe I'll find him when I least expect it," she told her friend.

"You always was picky," Mavis joked. "I wouldn't have let that sailor go, you know, the one who told you about Jamaica and all that. He was so good looking and you let him walk off."

"Nothing further from my mind that night," she reflected. "I was so young then; we both were. Looking back, I might have fallen for the Canadian guy had I ever seen him again. Fate didn't smile kindly on me that night." Her voice was low.

Mavis guessed what was going on. "I know," she said gently. "But we're here now and have a bright new future to look forward to. As far as I can see, that bloomin' war made women out of girls and men out of boys. That's something for us to be proud of. Now, when shall we meet up?"

"I'm free anytime," Emma told her. "Will your hubby...you haven't told me his name..."

"Carlo..."

"Won't Carlo mind if you go out without him? I'll make sure you're home before midnight," Emma joked.

"No, he won't mind, but I'll have to check his shifts and make sure he'll be able to look after Rico..."

Emma gasped audibly. "Rico? You already have a little boy? My goodness, Maeve, you have been busy!" Both girls laughed, turning back the years and recalling when they used to laugh at the silliest things as they were growing up.

"I know," Mavis agreed. "Two babies in two years. Not bad going for a girl who thought she would never have children. But that's another story for another time. Let's meet at the Red Lion. That way my mum will be there if I go into labour. How are your midwifery skills?"

"Hey, hold on a bit, Maeve. Are you likely to give birth any time soon?" Emma asked seriously.

"Relax, Em," Mavis said. "I was two weeks over my due date with Rico, so I can't see this one coming out on time. I'll give you a call when I've spoken to Carlo. See you soon. TTFN."

"Bye, Maeve. Look forward to it."

Eleven

"I think you are ready to manage your teaching practice, Mr Johnson," the tutor said at the end of the seventh week of training.

"Are you sure, sir? I mean, it has only been seven weeks," BJ answered.

"Yes, and this induction course has only one week left," the tutor told him. "You have coped easily with the method lectures and shown a great insight into the understanding of the English language. We have made sure you are able to impart your knowledge in interesting and entertaining ways. In my opinion, the pupils of Ashmore Street Primary School will benefit greatly with you as their teacher. Is there anything you are concerned about?"

BJ thought carefully before he spoke. "I do have one particular concern, if I might be honest with you, sir. I'm Jamaican, here in this country by invitation, but not everybody sees it that way."

"Ashmore Street has...if I might make so bold...a number of coloured children in the school community, children who came from Jamaica and Trinidad, the West Indies generally, with their parents who, in turn, hoped to find work and a secure future here for their children," the tutor explained. "It is for that reason my colleagues and I felt it would be in their interest and yours to give you that placement. The headmaster assures me that there have been no problems and let's face it, you and those children have much to offer with your experiences. Many of the children who were born here have never had the opportunity to travel around England, never mind going overseas. We are just trying to overcome the trials and tribulations wrought upon us by war. I have every confidence in you and you need not worry about the differences. We know the rapid training initiative is what we need in our education system; it was introduced with these situations in mind, but you already know all this, otherwise you wouldn't be here."

"Thank you, sir," BJ offered. "I shall do my best."

"And you won't worry about your ethnicity?"

BJ smiled. "No, sir, I won't. Onwards and upwards, as the saying goes."

~ * ~

The meeting with Mavis didn't happen until her husband, Carlo, was on an early shift, which meant he would be able to put little Rico to bed. "Don't be too late, *tesoro*," Carlo said as she left.

"I won't," she told him. "See you later."

"Drive *al cicero*," he called as she opened the door to leave.

His mix of English and Italian made her laugh. "I will," she reassured him. "I always do."

Emma and Mavis sat in an alcove not far from the bar. Mr Taylor was working the bar that night and he told Mavis he would keep a watchful eye on the two young ladies and keep them supplied with whatever drinks they required all evening.

"There'll be no alcohol for you, daughter of mine," he said seriously. "Bitter lemons all night. That's my grandchild you are carrying around with you."

"Oh, not bitter lemon, Dad!" Mavis cried. "It gives me heartburn something chronic! Fresh orange juice would be nice. Mum has some in the fridge upstairs if there's none behind the bar."

"I have some here for the gin drinkers," her dad said. "And what about you, Emma?"

"Just dandelion and burdock, thanks, Mr Taylor."

"Blimey!" Mr Taylor said. "The last of the big spenders! I'm not going to get rich off you two!" He laughed heartily. "And call me George, Emma. Nobody calls me Mr Taylor anymore. Everybody's my friend and I'm everybody's friend. Can't be any other way in a London drinking establishment!" He laughed again. "Ain't that right, Billy?" he asked the old man sitting at the far end of the bar.

"Yeah, that's right," Billy agreed. "Give us another 'alf, please, George."

"Coming right up. Tuppence-ha'penny, please."

After an hour of non-stop talking, Emma and Mavis were ready to replenish their glasses for the third time. "I'll go to the bar this time," Emma said. "Your dad is very busy and we can't expect him to keep coming over to give us personal attention."

"He won't mind," Mavis assured her.

"But I do," Emma said. "I would never expect anybody to wait on me hand and foot."

"Wait until you're pregnant!" Mavis quipped.

"In your dreams," Emma flashed back at her friend and took the half dozen steps to where she would buy the drinks.

Leaning casually on the bar, a very smartly dressed gentleman was standing alone. Emma particularly noticed him, because he was wearing a fashionable, light grey trilby hat to match his light grey pin-striped suit. As she stood on tip-toe to catch the barman's eye, she over-balanced and nudged the gentleman in the back. He turned to face her quickly.

For him, recognition was instant, and his face lit up with a beaming smile. "Hello again," he said cordially.

Emma looked at him questioningly. "Do I know you?"

"Not really."

"Well, why did you say hello again?"

The young man looked uncomfortable. "Sorry," he apologised. "I must be mistaken. I thought you were someone else."

"Is this man bothering you, Emma?" George asked from further along the bar.

"No," Emma was quick to answer. "It's okay, George."

Without taking much notice of Emma's reply, he turned to the young man and said bluntly, "Look, we don't want any trouble in here. I don't mind you having a quiet drink, but if you start bothering our girls, I'll have to put a sign on the door like some of the other city pubs have done. You know what I mean, son?"

The young man looked George in the eye. "I know exactly what you mean, sir, and I'm not here to cause trouble. I'll just finish my drink, then I'll leave."

"Yeah, that'll do just fine," George told him. "And just for the record, I don't want to cause trouble for you neither. Just be careful who you talk to. My advice to you is it might be best if you stick to your own kind."

The young man hastily finished his drink and went out of the pub. Emma looked at George, her eyes wide with disdain. She walked calmly towards the door, turned to look at George again, but he was busy serving Billy with another half-pint, completely oblivious of what he had just done with not a care in the world. When she was outside the door, she found the young man leaning on the wall with his hands in the pockets of his stylish suit, his head bowed as he studied his shoes. "Nice shoes," she commented, "But you'll spoil the cut of those trousers if you push your hands so deep in your pockets," she said cheerily.

The young man shrugged.

"Do you want to tell me what happened in there?" she asked.

The young man shrugged again.

Emma was undeterred and she leaned against the wall by his side. "Let's start again. You said hello as though you knew me. Why did you think that?"

The young man took a deep breath. "I stopped you from falling over when a big guy pushed his way down the gangplank of the *Windrush...*"

Emma smiled broadly with recognition. "So you did!" she exclaimed. "I should thank you again for that. Fancy your remembering me! You must have a good eye for faces." *This guy seems to be avoiding looking at me. What can have happened to make him so embarrassed?*

He took his hands out of his pockets and, offering his right hand to Emma he said, "I'm BJ..."

Emma took his hand. *Good, firm handshake, I like that.* "Nice to meet you, BJ. I'm Emma." *Look at that smile, but there's a look in his eyes I can't quite read.* Then out of the blue, she asked, "Shall we go for a walk along the high street and down towards the river?"

BJ looked stunned. "Er...er..."

"My goodness, I'm sorry. Did I say something to offend you?"

BJ's expression was one of puzzlement. "Are you aware what you have just asked?"

Emma cocked her head to one side and smiled, her eyes dancing with childlike mischievousness. "I'll just pop inside and tell my friend I'm calling it a night." She opened the door and purposely strode across to the alcove where Mavis was still sitting. "I'm going home now, Maeve. Thanks for a lovely evening. We'll do it again soon and let me know when the baby comes."

Mavis automatically looked at her watch. "We don't close until half-ten, Em. We have time for another drink before you go."

"I think I've had enough, thanks. There are no lavs in taxis and I have to get back to Windsor. Honestly, I'll give you a call." She found her friendliest smile and made sure it was in Mavis's direction. As she went through the door, she called, "See you soon. Promise."

Mavis looked wide-eyed at the door as it closed, sighed, and waddled up the stairs to say goodnight to her mother before she left too.

Emma found BJ still leaning on the wall, but not studying his shoes this time. As she approached him, he stood straight, touched his hat and said, "Hello again."

"Are we going for that walk or what?" she asked.

BJ smiled. "And I'll ask you again… are you aware of what you are asking?"

"Come on," she said. "We can talk as we walk."

"But—"

"No buts. Just put one foot in front of the other. It's easy. You'll soon get used to it," she told him.

"Are you always so bossy?" BJ asked.

"Only when it's necessary, and before you try to tell me it's frowned upon for a white woman to be seen walking out with a black guy, then I'll tell you it would be everybody else's problem, not mine."

BJ shrugged yet again, stuck his hands in his pockets and they set off in the direction of the river.

"If you were on the *Windrush*, you must have come in response to the government's request for strong, fit and healthy young men to help rebuild the motherland," she said. It was a statement, but it might have been interpreted as a question.

"I did, but I wasn't sure if I would be accepted since I'm not really a tradesman," he revealed. "Fortunately for me, the employment officer was more than helpful and he found me a place in a teacher training course. I would have done manual labouring work, but he seemed to think I would be better suited to a—"

"…To a white-collar job?" Emma interrupted.

"I guess so, but those are your words, not mine. I have to be very careful what I say," BJ admitted. "I don't like it, but I'm very aware that we stick out like sore thumbs in this community."

Emma touched his arm to indicate she wanted to stop walking momentarily. "Please don't let simple-minded people make you feel less than you are. It makes me so ashamed of my fellow countrymen who can't see the wood for the trees."

BJ was shocked. "What on earth are you saying? We are different, there's no getting away from that, but I just don't like being reminded of it every time I go out. I've always been a confident guy and a sensible one. Spending the last couple of months here in this strange land, it feels like my confidence is waning and sometimes I feel I'm becoming something I'm not." He paused and with a wry smile, slowly shook his head. "I've become a person I have recently named a *Devonite*." He smiled as he thought of his friend. *Sorry Devon. I'm not belittling you. You just needed to be shown the way.*

"A Devonite?" Emma questioned. "What has glorious Devon got to do with it?"

"Yeah, I've heard that Devon is beautiful and I intend to go there one day, but my friend who is called Devon is a young guy who arrived here at the same time I did, although I didn't know him previously. He was so brash and disrespectful when he landed that I cringed both for him and for me. He's a good kid really, but he had a massive chip on his shoulder and thought he was doing right in retaliating before he'd been attacked, for want of a better terminology."

Emma set off again at a slow pace and BJ followed. "I know somebody like that too," she admitted. *That sounds just like Leroy.* "What is Devon doing now?"

"He got a position in the Savoy as a trainee chef. That is quite something for him and I'm very proud of him," BJ told her. "He met a young girl in the food marquee at the shelter where we stayed when we first arrived. She seemed to have some influence over him. He hated the shelter until he met her, but I do worry he might be getting himself into a situation without realising it. And he won't be equipped to deal with it."

"What do you mean?" Emma asked.

BJ stopped and said clearly, "Look, Miss Emma—"

"Stop right there," she said abruptly. "I am Emma; Emma Louisa Williams to be exact. I don't require a title. What is it with you bl—?" She paused. "What is it with you guys that you need to assign a status to everybody?"

"It's our way, Miss Emma," BJ emphasised. "Manners, politeness, respect." He took a deep breath, and he felt his hackles rising. "I really don't know why I need to explain myself to you anyway. You are coming over as bossy and very opinionated. We have only just met and I don't wish to be rude, but why are you so interested?"

Emma suddenly went quiet. Her cheeks burned with embarrassment. She felt her stomach churn and her heart was going nineteen to the dozen. "I'm trying to be sociable, I guess..." *Oh my word! Nobody has stood up to me like that before. Why am I suddenly panicking? I'm tied up in knots inside. Suddenly this guy is turning my world upside down. He's handsome, intelligent, sensitive... Snap out of it, Emma. You are being ridiculous.*

"Are you all right, Mi... Sorry. Are you all right, Emma?" BJ asked.

It was Emma's turn to shrug without answering.

"Did I say something to upset you? I guess I didn't hold back just now."

Pulling herself together, Emma made an attempt at a sensible reply. "No, you didn't, and I'm sorry for being too forthright. One of my many failings. I am often told to think before I speak. Maybe I should get a taxi back home now. Thank you for your company. It was nice meeting you." *Stop gabbling, you idiot.* And she silently asked herself, *What on earth is happening?*

"It was nice meeting you, too," BJ agreed. "Maybe we can meet again sometime."

Emma was flustered. "Maybe ..." then, "Taxi!" she called as she hailed a very conveniently approaching cab. She opened the door quickly. "Twenty-one Castle Mews, Windsor," she instructed the driver and awkwardly flopped into the back seat.

BJ was confused but managed to wave as the taxi pulled away. *Now what was all that about?* he asked himself silently. *I never met anybody quite like her. What a complicated character; what a delightfully complex young lady she is.* He smiled to himself. *It takes all sorts to make a world, I guess...* He stopped in his tracks and looked around to make sure Emma had really left him standing there on the pavement. He dug his hands in his pockets again and strode confidently along the embankment to his one bed apartment in Brixton just a short walk from Ashmore Street where his new job was starting the following day.

Twelve

After a restless night, Emma woke still in complete confusion regarding her hasty retreat from BJ the night before. She went into the kitchen where her aunt was preparing breakfast and her father was sitting at the table reading his newspaper. Intermittently he grunted, but didn't look up when Emma appeared in front of him. "Good morning, you two," she said cheerily. "What is happening today?" She addressed them both, but gained little response.

After a minute or two, Auntie Edith said, "I might go into the city and meet my friend, Doris. Will you be okay to stay with your dad for a while?"

Emma was taken aback. "Er...er..." she mumbled.

"I won't go if you have plans."

"I have no plans, but..." *Oh my goodness. Am I really the person for this job?* "I haven't looked after him on my own before," she said and her thoughts were running away with her. *He hasn't spoken to me at all since I arrived home. How am I supposed to look after a man who clearly has no respect for anybody or anything around him? I know he's my father, but—*

"But you found it easy enough to look after Mrs Thomson. Why would you be nervous about looking after your own father?"

"I don't know," she admitted. "To compare him with Merle is totally misplaced. *She* accepted me without knowing me, and he's my father, and he doesn't appear to accept me, nor even know who I am."

Suddenly a booming voice echoed around the kitchen. "I'm here, yer know!" he shouted loudly, even though he was sitting only a couple of feet away. "I can hear you. I'm not dumb!"

Emma was dumbfounded, and as her aunt was quick to react, Emma just stood and stared. The dutiful sister bent over until she was face to face with her momentarily agitated brother. "There, there, Jack. Don't worry. I'll stay with you..."

"No," he boomed again. "*She* can do it." And he immediately went back to his newspaper calmly, as though nothing had happened.

Emma was amazed. "What was that?" she whispered to her aunt.

"Just one of his little outbursts," Edith explained. "He won't even know he's done it. Don't let it frighten you."

Before she left, Edith showed Emma everything Jack might need. "He is sometimes very demanding, so don't be afraid if he starts banging on the table to attract your attention. You don't have to sit with him all the time. It seems he likes being on his own. The psychiatric nurse says that sometimes happens when they come home after being forced to share a very small space with up to twenty men. He'll tell you what he wants when he wants it. His bark is worse than his bite. Don't worry, Emma. You'll be fine."

Emma gave her aunt a hug. "I'll do my best, Auntie," she said. "He's my dad and, in spite of his rejection, I do love him."

~ * ~

Her expected ordeal with her dad didn't come to fruition. After he had read his newspaper, he manoeuvred himself into the drawing room, heaved himself, much to Emma's surprise, into the easy chair he had recently commandeered as his own, and instantly fell asleep. Just before Edith returned around lunchtime, he had actually called out, "Emma! Drink!" and she was so delighted that she went to hug him only to have her feelings dashed when he raised a powerful arm to stop her in her tracks. Nevertheless, she smiled as she gave him his mug of tea, and he took it without any fuss.

Emma wrote to Ann that evening...*My dad actually called out to me today,* she wrote. *He only wanted a drink, but it was the first time he'd said my name since I arrived back. It's a start, I guess.*

I wish we could meet for our chats, Ann. Even though I have reconnected with my bestie from before, it's not the same. You and I felt the closeness as soon as we met and I can tell you anything. With Mavis, well, I don't know anymore.

Life here, in general, has changed in numerous ways and I experienced something last night that shocked me. I never realised the extent of racial discrimination that exists in this country. I saw it last night aimed at a guy who arrived from Jamaica at the same time as I did...

Suddenly she felt her stomach lurch again. She stopped writing while she tried to assess how she was feeling. *It's that sensation again, but it doesn't feel scary like it did before. It's actually a feeling of excitement, something similar to how I used to feel on Christmas morning as a child.* She smiled and found herself picturing BJ preventing her from falling as they made their way down the gangplank of the *Windrush*. For a moment, he held her in his arms; the picture was all so clear in her head. *Oh, my good lord,* she thought. *I need to see him again...Then...don't be stupid. You don't even know his name. What does BJ stand for anyway?*

When she received a reply from Ann, she had forgotten she had tried to explain her feelings about BJ in her letter. *Sounds to me like this BJ guy has plucked at your heart-strings,* Ann wrote. *'Bout time you allowed yourself to fall in love, Williams! My advice to you is... just be careful, but if you can't be careful, name it after me! Hahaha!*

~ * ~

With her continuing struggles to reconnect with her dad, Emma made a concerted effort to try to do things she remembered he liked before war was declared. "Shall we go and do a bit of fishing today,

Dad?" she asked one Wednesday morning when her aunt had gone out on her regular jaunt to the city.

"No," he grunted.

"Well, is there anything you think you would like to do?" she asked.

"No," he grunted again.

Emma sighed. "Let me know if you think of anything," she said as she left the room, but her thoughts were becoming more and more irritated. *For Pete's sake, Dad, do something to help yourself. You have Auntie Edith and me running round after you like scalded cats and you were never like that with Mum. If anything, you were the one doing things to help make her life easier. What happened to you out there? Tell me so I can try to understand.*

"Emma!" he called.

Emma was momentarily overjoyed that he had again called her name, and she went quickly to see what her dad wanted. "Yes?" she asked, not hiding her delight, only to have her feelings immediately thrown back in her face a second time.

Jack glared and pointed to the floor where his book was lying.

Trying desperately not to lose her temper, Emma bent to retrieve the book. "Oh, you're reading *Nineteen Eighty-Four*. So much has been said about it in the *Times'* book reviews. I'm not sure I would like it," and grasping the opportunity for a conversation with her father, "Is it really about the authorities totally ruling the lives of people in 1984? Sounds really scary to me."

Jack grunted and seemingly snatched the book from Emma's hand. She smiled weakly. "Maybe I'll read it when you've finished it." *Failed again. God give me strength.*

Sitting in the garden later and feeling the warmth of the summer sun on her face, she read the local evening paper to catch up on what was happening in Windsor over the holiday weekend. *Hmm, brass band concert in the park on Saturday. I think I'll go to that. Maybe Kathleen from our coffee club will go with me. She's in a similar position to me looking after her frail mother. I'll give her a call later.* She read the paper from cover to cover, but something caught her eye on the next to last page. *SITUATIONS VACANT. I wonder what jobs are going. Maybe having a job will give me a reason to get up in the mornings. I don't think I want a job looking after somebody again, though. I need a complete change.* "Hmm, what's this?" she said out loud, and then read silently. *Capable person to carry out office duties. Windsor County Primary School. Apply in writing stating relevant qualifications. No experience necessary. Training will be given.*

Thirteen

Two weeks later, Emma had secured the clerical position in the local school. She had used her Higher School Certificate in secretarial studies to obtain the post, even though she hadn't even thought about it since she had taken the exam in the early days of the war. Her duties involved typing up lesson notes for the newly qualified teachers who had taken part in the training initiative offered to those who wished to become teachers after the hostilities. She also learned how to duplicate worksheets using carbon paper. It was a messy process and she often went home with blue fingers through handling carbon paper all day. She loved her job and she made new work friends who invited her out for meals or just for a coffee and a chat. Windsor had become a popular hub with a few cafés springing up in spite of rationing, so her social life seemed to have improved since she had landed back on home soil six months before. Her job also provided welcome relief from being home all day with a less than communicative father and a fussy, yet endearing, widowed aunt.

Her office was situated by the school entrance and so she became the first line of communication for various visitors. Her days were busy, but happy. Sometimes, teachers would send a child with a message and she often looked up from her typing to see the big inquisitive eyes of a small child peering through the window in the door. "Come in," she would call, and the child would cautiously open the door, walk shyly up to her desk and offer her a note from the teacher without saying a word.

Soon after nine o'clock one Monday morning, there was a gentle knock on her door and she looked up expecting to see a child holding up a piece of paper from a teacher, but strangely, she saw nobody. Cautiously, she opened the door and peered round to find a gentleman who had obviously stepped out of view after he had knocked to gain her attention. For a moment, time stood still.

"Good morning, Miss Emma! What a surprise to see you here."

Emma was momentarily stuck for words. Eventually, she found her voice and asked, "The surprise is all mine. What are *you* doing here?"

"I could ask you the same, but I am here to see Mrs Hopkins. I believe she is expecting me."

"She is?" Emma questioned, her voice manifesting itself in a mouse-like squeak and then, more professionally, she said, "She is. She told me earlier she was expecting a Mr Johnson. Is that you?"

BJ grinned. "It is," he confirmed. "Shall I wait here?"

Emma breathed in deeply to ascertain control over her thoughts and her actions. "Mrs Hopkins' office is down the corridor, second on the right. She will be waiting for you."

"Thank you." He strode confidently down the corridor as Emma peered round her office door, watching him until he disappeared into the headmistress's room.

~ * ~

What seemed like hours later, BJ waved as he left the building, but made no attempt to stop and speak to her. Within minutes, Mrs Hopkins appeared. "We have a new teacher starting next week. His name is Mr Johnson and he has come to us highly recommended.

We are also expecting several new pupils whose families are being re-housed in Windsor. They are members of our new immigrant society, so we need to treat them with the utmost respect..."

"I understand, Mrs Hopkins. I lived in Jamaica for four and a half years. I am able to relate to these people..."

"Indeed," Mrs Hopkins said. "Maybe we shall all look to you for advice when we need it."

Emma was confused. "Just be normal, Mrs Hopkins," she said cheerily. "They are people just like us, after all."

"Not quite like us, Miss Williams," Mrs Hopkins stated quietly, but Emma chose not to reply.

~ * ~

The next few weeks Emma and BJ maintained a professional relationship; good mornings and good afternoons, but noticeably to Emma, she hadn't been given the opportunity to wish him goodnight. BJ avoided one-on-one conversations. He often sent a child with a message if he wanted Emma to type up his lesson notes or duplicate the pictures he needed to use in his creative writing activities and sometimes to provide him with exercise books when children had filled theirs. When he appeared in her office one lunchtime, she was quite taken aback. "My goodness," she said, not hiding her surprise. "What's happened? You've always sent a child to do your errands. Nobody available just now?"

BJ walked around her desk, pulled her up from her chair and led her to where her coat was hanging on a hook behind the door. He took the coat and offered it to her. "Put on your coat, Miss Williams, bring your packed lunch and we'll go for a walk in the park."

Emma was shocked. "Excuse me, Mr Johnson, but it might not be appropriate for me to be taking my lunchbreak away from school premises."

"Are you saying you would prefer to eat alone or just that you would rather not have lunch with me?" BJ asked.

Stunned, Emma looked at him with questioning eyes, but remained silent. *Why now, BJ?* she thought. *I can't do this while I'm at work. I have been waiting for weeks for you to talk to me and, if I'm honest, my heart flips every time I see you, but having lunch with you in the middle of a school day would send me into a state of undeniable suspended animation. I'd never get through the afternoon in one piece...*

"Okay then," he said nonchalantly. "Message received." He put her coat back on the hook and turned to walk out through the door.

"BJ!" Emma called in a theatrical whisper. "Not here, not now. Meet me at the park entrance at four-thirty."

BJ didn't reply. Nor did he give any intimation that he had received the message loud and clear.

~ * ~

Emma arrived at the park a few minutes early, but BJ wasn't there. It was late January and the nights were drawing in fast. It was typical weather for an English January, cold, almost icy, but fortunately it was dry. She sat on a bench just inside the gates, her gloved hands clasped on her knees, held primly together, and she stared straight ahead so as not to appear to be searching the road she had just walked along for BJ to appear. *He's not coming,* she thought. *Damn!* And then she saw him, walking confidently towards her, displaying the same, warm, beautiful smile she remembered from when she literally fell into his arms on the gangplank of the *Windrush.*

"Sorry I'm late," he said as he approached her. "Mrs Hopkins wanted a report on my progress with the Atherton boy and the West girls. They are having some minor problems in settling in." He paused. "We really don't need to talk about work, do we?"

"No, we don't. Shall we walk a while?" Emma suggested. "It's too cold to sit here. We'll freeze to death!"

"Walking will be good," BJ confirmed. "This English weather has forced a massive adjustment on me. I've had to buy clothes I never owned before and I even have a hot water bottle when I go to bed at night!" He laughed. "Now I know what having cold feet means—literally, not metaphorically."

Emma was not ready for small talk. "We have seen each other every day for the past few months and this is the first time we have found…" She stopped deliberately, and then continued, "This is the first time we have *made* the opportunity to get to know each other."

"That's true," he agreed. "I have wanted to talk again ever since you retreated in a taxi that night at the Red Lion. We were getting along fine and then you—"

"I went all funny on you," Emma openly admitted.

"Well, you said it," he told her. "And *funny* peculiar, not *funny* ha-ha. You left me very confused, but then I realised you were perhaps uncomfortable walking out late at night with a guy you didn't know and a black guy to boot."

Emma gasped. "Well, how wrong can you be?" she stated indignantly. "True, I *didn't* and *don't* really know you, but the bit about the black guy is so far from the truth."

BJ said nothing in reply.

"I'm going to say this once and I would like you never to make me repeat it," she said firmly.

"There's that bossy streak again," he said and nudged her in the ribs playfully.

"Shush!"

"And there it is again!"

Emma conceded defeat in the bossy stakes. "Okay," she said resignedly. "I'll try to keep my tone friendly, but this is a subject I feel so strongly about. I had to explain it on several occasions when I was living in your wonderful Jamaica. When I speak to a guy, I do not see the colour of his skin; I see a person…his demeanour, his manner, his smile, the look in his eyes…"

"That sounds wonderful and I, for one, more than appreciate it. Any black guy would…"

"Yet I detect a *but* is coming…"

BJ stopped walking and looked directly into her eyes, noticing she shivered involuntarily. "It's a big *but,* and one you should be aware of. It is not that long ago in the whole scheme of things that white people treated black people with the utmost disrespect. Many of us have suffered the insulting onslaught of cruel, demeaning words from people who think we should be treated as second class citizens. I had it at school, at college, in the army and, occasionally, since I arrived here."

"You mean people have actually said these things to your face?"

BJ led her to a bench and invited her to take a seat. "If I'm honest about being here, not to my face, but I see it in their looks and their actions when they move away from me as though I have some deadly disease. Like that night in the Red Lion. That guy assumed I was harassing you just because I said hello."

Emma instinctively took his hand in hers. "I noticed that and I hope I put him straight. That was one of the reasons I left when *you* did."

"I did wonder about that, but felt I was being too presumptuous. I hoped that when I came here, people would be more accepting and would appreciate that we were here to help. After all, we have been invited here to help rebuild the country after the war. William Blake—"

"He's dead, isn't he?" Emma interrupted.

BJ couldn't help but laugh. "I saw the funny side of his name, too, but he was the Employment Officer who recommended me for a place in the teacher training initiative and he restored my faith in the paler members of the world's population."

Emma grinned and squeezed his hand and he smiled at her show of affection. "We do have some good ones, you know," she assured him.

"Bill Blake treated me with respect and I liked that," BJ told her.

"I like him already," Emma divulged. "It's very plain to see we need more William Blakes in this world. But—"

"Now you are offering a *but?*" BJ asked as he took Emma's free hand in his and moved closer to her.

"I was going to say—"

"Yes?" and he inched even closer to her.

"I was going to—" She closed her eyes as his lips met hers, kissing her gently, lovingly, tenderly. She sighed and rested her head on his shoulder. "You have no idea how long I have wanted you to do that," she whispered.

BJ smiled his special, now familiar, wonderful smile. "Really?"

Emma felt her cheeks burning. "You know when I ran away from you that night?"

BJ nodded, still holding her close. "I do. How could I forget?"

"Well, I'll try to explain, although I have been endeavouring to explain it to myself without much success until now. You must have done something or said something that pulled on my heart-strings and my insides were doing somersaults. I was so confused and had to get away as soon as possible. After that, I thought of you every day, but I didn't think I would ever see you again. When you turned up at school that day, my heart skipped a beat again, but you seemed to be so distant..."

"I felt I had to be," he told her. "In spite of what we think personally, I have detected some awkwardness when Mrs Hopkins speaks to me. She covers it well, and I know she appreciates me in a professional sense, but I don't think she's so sure socially."

"What makes you say that?" Emma asked.

"Because just before the Christmas break, I overheard her talking to Mrs Maguire, the reception class teacher, and it seems she was unsure what Jamaicans did for Christmas..."

"You are joking," Emma declared. "Surely she would have more sense than that."

"Well, I began to think she didn't arrange a staff Christmas dinner because of me. When teachers would be bringing partners to a social event, having me there might have been an embarrassment for her."

"Now that's ridiculous, BJ. I know for a fact we didn't have a staff dinner because of the rationing. It would have made demands on us all to donate coupons, and most of the teachers have families that need to be fed and have at least one present from Santa Claus. You and Leroy seem to be carrying a mighty big log between you on your shoulders!"

"Who is Leroy?" BJ asked. "Do I have competition?"

Emma laughed. "Not at all, even though he would have asked me out if I had shown some interest. Leroy is just a friend. He's living in my house while I'm over here..."

"You own a house in Jamaica?"

"I do, in uptown Kingston, but I didn't buy it. My employer, Merle Thomson, left it to me in her will, but that's a story for another time." She looked at her watch. "Goodness, it's six o'clock. I'd better go home before they send out the cavalry to find me."

BJ looked disappointed. "Do you live far away?"

"No, just in Castle Mews by the west entrance to the park."

"Ah yes, number twenty-one," BJ recalled.

"How do you know that?"

"The taxi? Have you forgotten? In your haste to get away, you blurted out your address to the driver."

Emma laughed. "I'm really not in a hurry to get away now. I'm just being sensible. I'll see you tomorrow. Don't be late!"

"Bossy boots," BJ quipped. "I wouldn't dare!"

"Cheeky!" Emma quipped back.

"Just before you go," BJ added, "Can I be serious for a moment?"

"You mean you haven't been serious for that past hour or so?" Emma asked, feigning disappointment.

"Not that, silly," he replied. "I think we should keep a low profile at work, don't you? I mean, in view of what we have been discussing, we wouldn't be favourably accepted as a couple, would we? Even you should see that."

"Unfortunately I do," she agreed. "Baby steps, I think, for ourselves as well as for them."

Fourteen

Travelling from Brixton to Windsor each day was taking its toll, especially in winter. BJ asked Mrs Hopkins if she knew of any rooming houses where he might stay while he looked for a bedsit or a flat in Windsor or surrounds.

"I'm not sure, Mr Johnson," she said guardedly. "You might look in the local paper. People who have rooms for such eventualities advertise in there, I think. It is really beyond the realms of my experience."

BJ tried to remain calm. "I'll do that," he told her. "In the meantime, I'll just have to keep travelling on the train, but I must admit it's becoming quite tiring."

"You are a young man, Mr Johnson," Mrs Hopkins replied dismissively. "I'm sure you will take it all in your stride."

"I'm sure I shall," BJ said. "Thank you for your help."

~ * ~

"She was so condescending," he told Emma. "I really don't know how I kept calm."

"You have to, BJ. You can't let her get under your skin—pardon the pun," she said quietly. They were sitting on their usual bench after work that day, the same as every other day when they felt they might meet undetected by prying eyes. "I'll help you find somewhere to live. You can't keep travelling day in, day out. If you found a bedsit or flat here, we wouldn't have to worry about what we do."

"I know," BJ agreed. "We'd still need to be discreet, but I want to kiss you without wondering if someone is watching us from behind the bushes; I want to hold your hand as we walk along; I want to—"

"I want all that so much, too," Emma whispered. "And I want to say all this out loud instead of whispering all the time for fear of somebody listening in."

"I love you, Emma."

"Oh my...Oh my..."

"Is that all you can say?" BJ asked, deflated after the declaration of his feelings.

"No...no, of course not," Emma blurted out. "It's just that nobody has ever said those three little words to me before and I have never said them back to anybody either, but I love you, too, BJ." Tears trickled down her cheeks. "Thank you for loving me."

"No need to thank me, darling Emma. You are so easy to love, but I wish we didn't have to be so secretive about it," he said.

"Me too," Emma responded. "Snatching an hour each day after work is no way to conduct a relationship. I want to show the world that we are proud to be together. Maybe we can throw caution to the wind and let everybody see us as we are."

BJ was wistful. "Not yet, Emma. Wait a little longer until people have grown used to seeing black faces in their community. We have to wear our sensible hats for the time being. I spoke to Devon last night. He told me he and Rose are going steady. Her parents don't mind and he's got a steady job, but—"

"That word again," Emma interrupted.

"I know, but he said he's had some abuse from people around Brixton. I hate that and I have already witnessed Devon's reactionary streak, so I hope he keeps his cool. I feel responsible for him in a way."

BJ shook his head. "But that kid has changed a lot in the last year. Good luck to him."

~ * ~

Come June 1949, BJ had rented a small apartment in Slough, just a couple of miles from Windsor and within easy reach of the school. He hadn't seen any other black faces in the town, but the man from whom he was renting the apartment was, himself, an immigrant from Poland and he told BJ he was very happy to be helping other immigrants get settled.

When he broke the good news to Emma, she was overjoyed. "That's wonderful," she enthused. "I'll help you move in. Have you much stuff?"

"Not much," he informed her. "Just a bed, a sofa and other bits and bobs. There is some furniture in there already...a dining table and four chairs, and a radiogram with a few records. The owner has put in a new gas cooker and there's a meat-safe in the pantry where it's cool. Devon's girlfriend's brother has a van and has agreed to help me. I think in the whole of London, Devon and I have found the only people who welcome us with open arms!"

"I told you there are some good ones," Emma reminded him. "We just have to educate the rest."

"Baby steps," BJ reminded her. "Baby steps and we'll hopefully get there in the end."

~ * ~

In the middle of nineteen forty-nine, Edith Booth bought a new Ford Anglia, her pride and joy. "Might as well put my land-army skills to good use. I wasn't there for very long, but they taught me to drive," she told Emma the day she announced she had invested in a motor car.

"You never told me you were in the land-army, Auntie," Emma said. "Fancy keeping that a secret!"

"It wasn't a secret, Emma. I don't think about it much. I joined towards the end of the war, not too long after you left for Jamaica," Edith divulged. "When your dad was brought home, I had to look after him. The war was practically over then."

"Merle taught me to drive and I still have the old jalopy in the garage over there," she told her aunt. "Leroy will look after it for me, but I doubt there's much life left in it by now. Mind you, he's a motor mechanic so maybe he can work miracles on it. Your Ford Anglia is luxurious by comparison."

The day BJ was moving into his flat, Emma asked if she might borrow the car as she was helping her friend from the coffee club move to a new house in Slough. "I want to make a pie for lunch. She has her brother and his friend helping too, and I said I'd make sure they had something to eat," she lied.

"That's very generous of you, dear," her aunt said. "There isn't a lot of meat in the butcher's, though. We have the flour and lard for the pastry, but it might be more of a potato pie than a meat and potato one."

"I'll nip down early and hope I'm the first in the queue," Emma said in an effort to stop herself from blushing at her barefaced lies.

"Good idea and you will take care with my car, won't you? I feel it's like allowing you to look after my child for the day."

"Of course," Emma assured her. "I shall drive very carefully, I promise. Oh, and thank you, Auntie Edith. I love you."

Edith flushed on hearing those words of endearment. "It's a long time since anybody said that to me. Thank you, dear."

Emma smiled. "You're welcome."

~ * ~

Managing to buy half a pound of minced beef, Emma made the pie she had promised BJ and filled it out with lots of potatoes and carrots. Cooking the mince in Oxo stock and boiling the potatoes and carrots together while she made the pastry, her heart was racing at the thought of seeing BJ in his new home. *How wonderful to be able to relax instead of worrying about whether anybody has seen us together. I hate myself for being so secretive, but I'm sure it's for the best. Neither of us wants to lose our jobs and we can't be sure we wouldn't be publicly ostracised knowing what many people think of black people living amongst us.* She sighed deeply.

"That was a deep one," her aunt commented just as Emma closed the oven door to bake her pie.

"Oh, I didn't see you there, Auntie."

"Are you worried about something? You gave a sigh as though it were coming from the bottom of your soul," Edith commented.

Emma thought quickly. "No, I'm not worried about anything except I need this pie to be ready like ten minutes ago. I promised I'd be there for twelve-thirty and it's half past eleven already. I just need to change into slacks and a blouse in case I can help to carry anything or put up curtains."

"Slough is only just down the road really, so I'm sure you'll be there on time," Edith told her. "Go and get changed and I'll keep an eye on the pie while you're upstairs. Where in Slough is this house?"

Oh heck! Think quickly. "I think it's not too far from the station," Emma said. "Langley Road."

"That's nice," Edith replied. "Off you go now and get changed. I'll watch your pie doesn't burn."

At five minutes past twelve precisely, Emma wrapped her pie in two tea towels to keep it warm and placed it on the floor of the car at the passenger side. She set off from Castle Mews, making sure she was clear in her mind where she was going. *Left at the end of the road; second right, and then straight on for two miles to the T-junction; right into Langley Road, and look for a large Victorian property, number one hundred and forty-eight; first floor, flat three. I'm sure I can't miss it. There'll be several people coming and going.* She smiled to herself. *And at least two black faces!*

Much to her surprise, BJ, Devon, Rose and her brother, Fred, were sitting on the front steps of the house as she pulled up. BJ stood as she got out of the car and ran to greet her. "You're here!" he cried. "I'm so pleased to see you." He didn't hug her and she desperately wanted to give him a kiss, but she held back.

"This is Emma," he said, introducing her to his friends. "And these people are Rose, Devon and Fred."

"Hello," Emma beamed. "Pleased to meet you. I've heard—"

BJ was quick to interrupt. "That pie smells delicious. Let's go inside and eat. Rose, will you show Emma where everything is kept?"

"You must have been very busy if you've finished already," Emma observed. "I thought I would be helping to hang curtains and the like."

Rose turned as she climbed the stairs to the first floor. "We were here by seven-thirty. We packed up the van last night and BJ stayed at ours so we could make an early start."

The boys hung back and Devon was the first to speak. "You got a good one there, BJ. Well done you!"

"What do you mean?" BJ asked guardedly. "Emma just works at the school. She offered to help and bring us some lunch."

"Who do you think you are kidding, BJ?" Devon chided. "Anybody can see it a mile off. The way you look at each other speaks volumes."

BJ was surprised at Devon's powers of observation. "Damn," he snapped. "We don't want to go public yet. It's important we tread carefully, especially when we are at work."

"Why?" Devon asked bluntly.

"You know why, Devon. I've told you often enough. We have to keep a low profile until the great British reserve knows we are no threat."

"Speak proper English, BJ," Devon pleaded. "You know I don't understand all that clever language of yours."

BJ playfully punched Devon's arm. "Don't rock the boat," he said. "I know you understand what *that* means." They laughed together and Fred stood by without contributing to the discussion.

"But look at Rose and me," Devon added. "We don't mind who sees us as a couple, and Fred is happy with it, aren't you, Fred?"

"Yeah," Fred offered, but gave no other opinion.

"And so are Rose's ma and pa," Devon added. "It's just ignorant people who think they know us, and they don't. I've grown a thick skin, I can tell you."

Suddenly Rose was calling from upstairs. "Come on, you lot. Lunch is on the table. Come and eat it while it's warm."

After lunch, the three helpers took their leave. "Thanks so much for all your hard work, guys. I couldn't have done it without you," BJ told them as he and Emma waved them off.

"What are friends for?" Rose offered without reservation. "See yer later, guys."

Fifteen

Emma washed the dishes and BJ dried them and put them away. "I'll give you a quick tour when we've finished here," he said.

"Okay," Emma said enthusiastically. "I'm impressed with what I have seen so far. You must be paying a pretty penny for it...not that I'm prying."

"I had to put down ten pounds as a bond and then I pay five pounds a month, which includes gas and electricity. I think that's very reasonable, don't you?"

"It sounds reasonable to me," Emma agreed.

"The landlord told me that rent is dearer the nearer to London we are. I don't think I could afford to live in the city. The council paid my rent in Brixton, but only until I earned enough to rent for myself," BJ explained. "Shall we have a cup of tea? I've become very English in the past couple of years. I have drunk enough tea to sink a ship!"

"Tea would be nice, but show me round your new home first, BJ," she suggested. "I'm so excited for you."

"Well, you've already seen the living room and the kitchen, but you have to look at the pantry. It's enormous and the meat safe is big enough to hold all my fresh groceries and milk, well, what my coupons will allow me to buy. It's one of those cream and green metal ones and has drawers for cutlery and kitchen utensils too."

Emma grinned. "My, my," she said with a twinkle in her eye. "You have gone up in the world. And look how well stocked your pantry is!"

BJ grinned. "I've been saving some of my coupons each week to buy what I could afford. I wanted to have something to eat at least for this week before I need to go shopping again."

Emma smiled at him admiringly. "You are so organised and methodical, BJ. I like that in a man..."

"And you know other men who aren't?" he asked, flirting with her a little.

"Well...I know Earl Brown is particular about how he organises his garage," she said, returning the flirtatious tone.

"And who might Earl Brown be?" BJ enquired. "Do I need to be concerned? First Leroy and now Earl."

"He's my best friend's husband in Kingston. He's ex-army, and his training has made him very methodical in the way he does things," Emma remarked as BJ led her to the room he had made into his study.

"Like this?" he asked, opening the door, revealing a desk with an angle-poise lamp and a leather-bound blotting pad with matching pen and pencil tray taking pride of place.

"Gee!" Emma exclaimed. "You sure are organised and look at that bookcase! How have you acquired so many books in such a short time?"

"I packed them up before I left and asked my brother to send them when I found a job," BJ revealed.

"You have a brother?"

"I have a brother and a sister living in Barbados now," he disclosed. "Both are married with children. I'm the oldest, the most organised and, I think, the most ambitious."

"I have to say that you are certainly ambitious and you appear to be very organised," she told him.

"The army does that to a guy…"

Emma took his hand. "You have never told me about your army days," she said gently. "Are they something you'd prefer to forget? I can't see my dad ever telling us what happened in Italy, but I can't see him forgetting what his time in the army has done to him either…" She took a deep breath and said through her tears. "He's only half the man he was. Well, not even a half, if I'm honest."

BJ took her in his arms and held her close. "I'm sad for him and for you," he whispered into her hair. "You smell delicious."

Somehow while talking about being organised and methodical, they had made their way into the bedroom. "And this is where I sleep."

Somewhere above her head, way up in the ceiling, she heard BJ's voice, thick and sensual. "I love you, my darling Emma. I love you so much." He tightened his hold, feeling the curves of her delicate frame.

Her thoughts came fast and wild. *Oh my dear, dear BJ. Is this going to be my moment of ecstasy? How do I tell you? I'm twenty-eight years old and I have never had…* "I love you, too." The words came out of her mouth, but they sounded to her as though they were miles away.

BJ groaned. "Oh, Emma, Emma…"

She pushed him away and felt her heart beating fast as she looked longingly into his eyes.

BJ looked at her. "What is it?" he asked. "Are you saying no?"

Breathing in deeply, she bowed her head, unable to continue looking into his eyes.

BJ asked again, "What is it? Are you saying no to me? Tell me please, Emma."

She dared to look at him again and she saw the look of rejection in his eyes. "I'm not saying no…I'm not …please believe me, but…"

"So what is bothering you?"

"Promise you won't laugh, or smirk, or gasp, or…"

BJ was puzzled. "Did I misread the signs? If so, I'm sorry. You just told me you love me…"

"And I do, truly I do, but…" *Just tell him, you idiot.* "I've never done it before. I'm twenty-eight years old and still a virgin."

"Ohhh," he sighed. "You had me scared for a moment. If you're not ready, I understand. We can wait until—"

Without thinking more about it, she automatically grabbed at his sweater and pulled it over his head and, at the same time, he unbuttoned her shirt revealing small, but firm and perfect breasts in a delicate lace bra. His breathing was fast and heavy and they grabbed at each other's clothing until they lay naked on the bed.

Afterwards, happy and sated, they held each other close until their breathing was normal again. BJ was the first to speak. "I love you," he told her again. "I have never loved this way before. You are a gift from God. I think I loved you when you accidentally fell into my arms as we were disembarking from the *Windrush*. Fate certainly played a winning hand for us that day." He stroked her hair, her back, her breasts, her thighs. "Beautiful," he mused. "So beautiful."

Emma took his face in her hands and kissed his lips gently. "Thank you," she whispered.

"For what?"

"For loving me that way."

"For me there is only one way to show how much I love you. Saying it only *tells* you; making love *shows* you, one soul fulfilling another soul, two hearts entwined and beating as one, one's inner being meeting another's inner being in passion and loving abandonment...a celebration of life as we know it."

"Wow!" she gasped. "You should write a novel. How wonderful to be able to express yourself like that."

"Well," BJ said. "You have now touched on another aspect of my life I haven't talked about. I was a writer of sorts in Jamaica."

"I see," she said admiringly. "You certainly have the talent for it. What did you write?" She sat up, pulled the sheet up to her chin and rested her chin on her knees.

"Well, there's the rub," he explained. "I had just been asked by the local newspaper to write a column about being a war correspondent—retrospective, of course—and I was going to accept until I saw the invitation to come over here."

"Wouldn't it have been easier to stay at home and write?" Emma asked.

"It certainly would, but then I would never have met you."

"And looking at it another way, you wouldn't have had to put up with narrow-minded bigots who seem intent upon making your life a misery," Emma offered.

BJ sat up to join her, placed his arm around her and, as she rested her head on his shoulder, he said firmly and clearly, "I can safely say that what I have now by far out-weighs sitting behind a desk in the searing heat in a newspaper office where every man and his wife seem to smoke. I would have died from lung cancer, or boredom, whichever got me first."

"That sounds awful," Emma declared. "But I thought there was very little evidence that cigarettes are the cause of lung cancer."

"So the manufacturers say, but they would, wouldn't they? If everybody stopped smoking, they'd be out of business," BJ stated. "I think I believe medical evidence rather than the opinions of money driven businessmen."

"Well, that tells me then!" Emma said smiling. "And just for the record, I'm with you. I have never smoked and I don't think I ever shall. The mere thought of sucking in all that smelly smoke turns my stomach."

"I tried when I was overseas during the war, because everybody was smoking and it was something to do while all the war correspondents waited for the next assignment..."

Emma sat bolt upright. "You were actually at the Front?" she asked in dismay.

"Only right at the end of the war," he told her. "I enlisted quite late by comparison with others. The pacifist in me ruled my actions for a while. There was no conscription for us and we knew only too well about segregation still evident in the States and many of us stayed back on moral grounds. When we were more or less assured that Hitler was finished, the final onslaught never came for the late enlisters. I was sent to Bergen-Belsen to report on what was happening there."

Emma took a sharp intake of breath. "That must have been terrible," she said. "I can't imagine how you would feel reporting all that horror for people like me to read. I ran away from the Blitz to find some sort of solace in this mad, mad world. Those poor people never had a chance of escaping."

"It wasn't good and I must admit I crumbled under the strain..." He paused while he regained his composure. "I rarely think of it. I have to block it out to survive."

"I understand..."

"That's why coming here instead of recounting all that stuff for newspaper readers was easy," he said. "And meeting you has been a very welcome bonus."

"A bonus, hey?" Emma asked coyly. "I've only heard of bonuses applied to wages. I know we work in the same school, but please don't treat me as part of your salary."

BJ grabbed hold of her and they finished up rolling around on the bed, laughing happily in their loved-up state. "It's seven o'clock, Emma," he suddenly announced.

"Oh no!" she cried. "I promised Auntie Edith I'd be home by six." She hurriedly put on her clothes and BJ lay on the bed, watching her as she dressed.

"I love you," he told again.

"I love you too," she replied. "But I have to fly. I would hate to invite too much questioning when I get back."

BJ sat up and grabbed his robe. "Will you be questioned?" he asked, his tone serious.

"Probably," she admitted. "It's the first time I have borrowed her car, and I know she was a bit worried about it. I don't want to blot my copy book, or she won't lend it to me again."

"When will I see you again?" he asked.

"Monday at work. I can't lie again tomorrow. My auntie's not dumb and she picks up on any little incongruity, especially with me."

"But I can't go a whole day without seeing you," he pleaded.

"Baby steps," she reminded him. "Much as I want to be with you, we agreed that baby steps was the way to go. Don't let's make it hard for each other." She blew him a kiss and left.

Standing at the window of his new apartment, BJ watched as she drove off. He smiled to himself. *I wonder what happened to that cup of tea...*

Sixteen

The lovers felt they would manage their lives without hindrance. In school, they hardly acknowledged each other and hoped they didn't draw attention to their flourishing relationship. They left school at different times and took the train to Slough. BJ had a key cut for Emma so she could come and go as she pleased. Whoever arrived home first put the kettle on and prepared to make tea as soon as the other arrived. The routine would always be the same. Cup of tea, make love, have a short while wallowing in each other's company, then say *au revoir* until the next day.

"It has to be *au revoir*," Emma insisted. "Goodbye is too final and I couldn't bear to say goodbye to you...ever."

The first couple of days of their well-planned routine passed without problem. On the third day, she arrived home later than usual, her aunt questioned her. "Why are you suddenly arriving home late, Emma?"

Alarm bells ringing, Emma looked at her aunt whose expression told her she wasn't too pleased. "I have decided to finish my typing assignments and all the duplicating at the end of each day," she blatantly lied. "I have found it much better that I start with an empty desk when I arrive the following morning. My work begins to pile up even before school starts and some of it that comes in during the day is needed first thing the following morning. So far it seems to have worked..."

"Sounds silly to me," Edith stated matter-of-factly. "I think I'd prefer to go in earlier each morning than staying later at night."

"Why are you so concerned about it, Auntie?" Emma asked, trying to keep her tone amicable. "We don't eat until seven and I'm always home by then."

Edith pursed her lips as though she were about to embark upon some sort of crusade. "You are becoming a little selfish, don't you think?"

Emma was startled. "How do you mean, selfish?" she asked, still trying to stay calm. *Please don't upset my life, Auntie. I...*

"I mean I would like some help with dinner occasionally and your father grows more demanding by the day. Since you got that job at the school, we see you less and less. You may as well be living elsewhere. God knows you don't appear to be happy living here anymore."

Emma stood still and stared at her aunt who was delivering an oratory verging so near to the truth. "I'm sorry," she said. "I really don't know what to say. You are clearly distraught about it. Are you suggesting I find somewhere else to live? I pay for my keep here, so paying rent somewhere else wouldn't be very much different for me, but you might miss that little bit of income. If it's a matter of finances..."

Edith continued, unrelenting. "It's not about money, Emma. Most young ladies of twenty-eight would be married by now and have a couple of children. You never mention that you have male friends, but you go out each weekend with this girl, Kathleen, from this group you call a coffee club, yet you never invite her here for coffee; in fact, we never see any of your friends..."

"Hold on, Auntie. What is this? A lay-into-Emma day?" Emma asked, now allowing her tone to display her aggravation. "Why the sudden assassination of my character? As you say, I am twenty-eight years old and, as such, I think I'm entitled to a private life without advertising every minute detail of my actions and my whereabouts. I don't invite Kathleen here for morning coffee or afternoon tea since it smacks of middle-aged women and dowager ladies who have nothing to talk about except other people's business." *Auntie Edith has touched a nerve and I don't mind admitting it. I have just found the love of my life and I want to shout it loud and clear to the world, but that world has so much prejudice so I can't!* "If you would prefer, I will start looking for somewhere else to live to prevent being questioned every time I come home. Will that satisfy you?"

Edith removed a lace-edged handkerchief from her apron pocket and dabbed her face affectedly. "You are just like him in there," she cried. "I'm worn out being at his beck and call and you don't seem to care anymore. You spend all your time at this job you have. You seem to be running away just like when you ran off to Jamaica."

Emma bent her head to hide her guilt. "I understand, Auntie, I do, and I admit I feel guilty about leaving Dad with you day in and day out." She paused, took a deep breath and started again with more consideration for her aunt's feelings. "Maybe we should try to do something that will give *him* a break from us. We have tried, you particularly, to look after him as best we can, but I'm sure there is help to be gained from the British Legion or other military institutions."

"You mean bundle him off to a care home?" Edith said. "I don't think he'd like that."

"He doesn't like anything anymore, does he?" Emma stated firmly. "Maybe, *just maybe*, he might like being amongst men who have all been in the same boat. I think that will be good for him," Emma suggested. "I'll see what I can find out, but we won't say anything until we know what it entails."

~ * ~

Trying to juggle work, home, and BJ was more difficult than she had imagined. "I'll have to try and go home early some evenings after work, BJ," she said. "Auntie Edith has suddenly become bad tempered and I'm not helping with spending all my spare time with you."

"I hear you, Miss Emma..."

She gave him a steely look.

He grinned in his own inimitable way. "I hear you, Emma, but how else can we spend time together?"

Emma sighed. "I don't know, love, but we need to find an easier way that doesn't make me tell lies all the time. I'm becoming quite an adept liar and I hate it. I was always honest with myself and with others."

BJ walked over to the window and without turning to face Emma, he said. "Let's tell everybody..."

"Are you kidding me?" she asked. "Have you thought about the consequences if we do?"

BJ turned slowly to find Emma's whole being overwhelmed with concern. "I want to hold you close and tell you everything will be all right," he said as he moved towards her, but she simultaneously moved away from him. "Emma?" he asked gently. "What is this?"

She looked into his eyes, big brown eyes that showed all the emotions she, herself, was feeling inside. "Don't hold me, BJ, because if you do, I won't be able to think sensibly. Every time you touch me, I want more. My feelings for you cloud my judgment. Your touch drives me crazy and feeling your breath on my face makes me—"

"And what's so bad about that, my darling?" he asked and took another step nearer.

"No, BJ, don't come any nearer. We have to be serious about this. Let's sit at the table, opposite each other as though we are having a meeting. No touching and no declarations of love...just for now."

BJ frowned, but did as he was asked. He kept his hands clasped on his knees under the table in order to resist the urge to reach across and touch her. "Please, Emma, don't make this harder than it needs to be. The future is going to be what we make it."

"But it *is* hard, BJ," she cried. "The baby steps we agreed to take are suddenly becoming giant strides and I'm not sure I am ready to walk confidently in the present, never mind into the future."

"Look," he asserted. "Our love is strong...new, but strong and powerful. Love in its infancy always dictates the passion we feel more than we will experience when we have grown used to each other. The sexual urgency we are feeling at present cannot naturally keep going with that overpowering necessity we are consumed by just now."

"I said no declarations of love, BJ," Emma reminded him. "This is not an assessment of how much we love each other, and you know it. We...and I think I can speak for us both in this respect...we want that love to survive in a world of narrow-minded individuals who think that the colour of one's skin is a sign of one's class. It's class distinction at its worst."

BJ sighed. "There will always be those people, Emma. My people have experienced prejudice all their lives in one form or another. What makes you think you can single-handedly make them accept people for whom they are, rather than judge them, often wrongly, because of the colour of their skin? There are good and bad in all races, but according to newspapers, any crime committed must necessarily be the actions of black men. That's the unfair nature of the beast."

Emma tried to stop her tears, but they came anyway. "But we belong together, BJ. We are Romeo and Juliet, Lancelot and Guinevere, King Edward and Wallis Simpson. They managed to stay together against the odds."

"Not without a fight, darling. Not without standing up to those who opposed them," BJ informed her. "That's what we'll have to do if we are to be together for ever."

"I want to belong to a society where there is no antagonism, no judgment, no prejudice."

"Belonging is all we ask for," BJ said sadly.

"Is that too much to ask?" she queried.

BJ sighed; a long, deep sigh that showed the depth of his feeling. "I'm afraid it is, darling. I'm afraid it is."

Seventeen

Edith Booth sat staring at her cup of tea until it went cold. She took a sip, grimaced, stormed to the kitchen sink and forcefully threw the tea down the drain. The tea splashed the window, the draining board, the floor and her white blouse. "God almighty!" she cursed. "That just about sums up my life at the moment. All over the place, no proper focus and too much responsibility for a woman of my age."

"Edith?" came the roaring voice from the sitting room.

She ignored it.

"Edith!" more loudly now.

She still ignored it.

All at once, there was a thunderous crash, and Edith went running into the sitting room to find tea splattered around the room, the majority of it running down the door and a smashed mug in numerous pieces on the carpet.

"What the hell is happening, Jack?" she berated.

"Cold tea," Jack complained loudly, his usual petulance securely in place.

Edith stood and stared at him, her breathing coming in short gasps and her heart seemingly thumping at her breastbone. Suddenly she found her voice. "The whole world does not revolve around you, Jack Williams. I can't do this anymore. You have tried my patience for too long and it's time you listened to the truth. You aren't my responsibility. That daughter of yours does nothing to help and I know she's lying to me about working late. I just need to prove it, and mark my words I will prove it, whatever it takes." She took a deep, deep breath and continued. "You, my man, will have to go where the professionals can look after you. I've done my whack…" She was screaming like a banshee and sobbing from the bottom of her soul.

"Shut up!" Jack shouted back. "Shut your bloody mouth!"

The shock of her brother's words caused her to stop her tirade. Quieter now, she said calmly, "The British Legion assessors are coming this afternoon. I've told them I can no longer look after you."

~ * ~

"Your dad is moving out next weekend," Edith told Emma when she arrived home from work.

"That's it then?" Emma asked belligerently. "A *fait accompli*? No consultation? You went to see them behind my back?"

Edith was firm and stood her ground. "I did," she confirmed. "You said you'd look into it, but you didn't. You are always too busy doing whatever it is that demands your attention every evening. I took it upon myself to go to the British Legion headquarters and explained the situation. They were very sympathetic towards me…"

"What about me?" Emma asked.

"There you go again, Emma; as selfish as ever," Edith scolded. "I told them you weren't prepared to give Jack full time care…"

"Oh, thanks for that," Emma replied sarcastically.

Edith walked into the kitchen and Emma followed. "You know, young lady," Edith continued unabashed, "you don't know how lucky you are. You take everything for granted and since you came back from Jamaica, you have had everything given to you on a plate. Show some gratitude instead of taking what you can get all the time and giving nothing in return."

Emma stood quietly and listened shamefacedly. *She's right too. I have to admit I have thought of nothing but BJ for the past few months. He's my world and I can't live without him. I know I should have been helping Auntie Edith, but my heart is ruling my head...*

"Have you nothing to say for yourself, Emma?" her aunt asked, still with anger in her tone, breaking Emma's train of thought.

"I'm sorry," Emma whispered.

"Sorry isn't good enough, my girl," Edith spat. "You and your father have brought out the worst in me. I have never had to speak like this to anybody in all my life. I don't know about your dad needing psychiatric care; I think I need it, too." She threw up her arms in despair and stormed out of the kitchen, stomped up the stairs and into her bedroom, slamming the door hard behind her.

Emma walked slowly and cautiously into the sitting room where her dad was sleeping in his chair, oblivious of the fracas that had been filling the house for the past half an hour. She sat opposite him on the sofa and talked very quietly, hardly above a whisper. "You and I have caused a lot of trouble for Auntie Edith, you know. I have so wanted to talk to you about what is going on in my life. I could always do that before..." She paused poignantly. "...before you went to war. When Mum told me off about something, you would take me into your potting shed and try to explain what I had done wrong. Then you would ruffle my hair and call me your little princess..." She wept openly. "Oh Daddy, what has become of you?" She paused and asked herself silently, *What has become of me?*

~ * ~

The following day, Emma beckoned to BJ as he walked past her office. "I need to talk to you urgently," she told him.

"Not here, Emma. We agreed."

"It has to be now," she said forcibly. "I can't see you this week other than at school. No arguments, please. Just take my word for it."

"Excuse me?" BJ remonstrated. "Why?"

"Not now, BJ. We have work to do," she said firmly, then seeing the look of devastation in his eyes, she added, "Big trouble on the home front."

The worried look on his face haunted Emma throughout the day. When home time came, she looked down the corridor towards BJ's classroom, but he was nowhere to be seen.

Her aunt was surprised to see her soon after four o'clock in the afternoon. "Oh," she said as Emma walked through the door. "Nobody needs their work completing for tomorrow morning?"

"I decided to leave it today," she told her aunt. "After yesterday, I figured you needed a bit more help and you were right, I have been selfish. I was putting other people before my family."

"Well, thanks for that at least, my dear," Edith said. "I didn't tell you earlier, but I saw the doctor yesterday morning and he said I had to start thinking of myself for a change, otherwise I would certainly have a nervous breakdown..."

Emma was shocked. "Oh, Auntie, I'm so sorry..."

"I think I literally had that breakdown yesterday," Edith explained. "I didn't take the tablets he prescribed until I stormed off, four instead of two, and I slept right through to nine o'clock this morning. Thanks for giving your dad his breakfast..."

"That's the least I could do under the circumstances," Emma said. "I was afraid to waken you before I went to work. I wasn't sure if you were staging a protest or not." She dared to smile in her aunt's direction.

"Maybe storming off to my room was the protest," Edith admitted. "But let's try and get along and make a bold effort to see that your dad gets settled in The Willows as soon as possible."

"Does he know he's going there?" Emma asked.

"I told him he was going in there to convalesce," Edith pointed out. "He didn't explode, so I think he approves. Who knows what's going on in that brain of his? I have to convince myself that it will be best for him. My conscience sometimes gets in the way of making sensible decisions."

Emma gave her aunt a hug. "I'm sure it will be and we can visit him regularly. It isn't that far to Southend, is it?"

Four days without being with BJ was a real strain. She winked at him when he walked past her office and he grinned in his own inimitable way. At lunchtime, she called her aunt. "Do you mind if I come home late today? My work is piling up with going home early each day. It's Friday, so I'll get it all done for Monday morning.

"No, that's all right, dear. Your dad's things are all packed up ready for tomorrow, so when the Warrant Officer comes to pick him up, all we have to do is wave him off. I know I shouldn't say this, but I am feeling the relief already."

"I'm pleased for you and thanks, Auntie. You are so kind."

When four o'clock came, Emma was ready to leave immediately so that she might catch the early train and surprise BJ when he arrived home. She would have tea ready and then she would be able to tell him her secret. She was sure the last week's morning nausea would disappear once she had given him her news.

~ * ~

Edith Booth was shopping in the village just before half past five that evening. She had met her friend, Doris, for afternoon tea and then gone to the grocery store with her list of items she needed for the following week. As she left the shop, she looked at her watch. *Five-fifteen,* she silently acknowledged. *I'll call in at the school and give Emma a ride home.* She met the school caretaker at the door. "Is Miss Williams ready to leave?" she asked him.

"Well now," he said. "She already left soon after four. I saw her walking towards the station as I arrived to do my cleaning."

"Are you sure?" Edith asked.

"Absolutely, Mrs. Abso-bloomin'-lutely," he confirmed. "There's only one young lady like her on the staff. I couldn't mistake her for anybody else."

Edith was confused. *Now where can she have gone? Looks like she's playing her little games again. Hmm. I can be as cute as you, Emma Williams. Just you wait and see.*

Eighteen

BJ looked up at his window as he arrived home from work. The curtains were open. *That's odd,* he thought. *I'm sure I left them closed this morning. I didn't want the afternoon sun to damage the polish on my new desk.* He opened the front door and bounded up the stairs two at a time. He went to put the key in the lock of the apartment door, but it was ajar. *What the hell is going on?* He cautiously pushed on the door and sidled in to ascertain what was happening inside, panic raging in his chest.

"Surprise!" Emma called as soon as she saw him.

BJ dropped his briefcase before he ran up to her and swept her off her feet into his arms. "Why didn't you tell me you were coming today?" he asked.

"And spoil the surprise?"

BJ laughed. "And what a wonderful surprise!"

"I've boiled the kettle," she told him. "We'll have a cuppa and talk a while. I have so much to tell you."

"And I have very little to tell you except that I love you and I have missed you so much this week," he said lovingly. "Every day has been forty-eight hours long for me."

Emma explained about the almighty row there had been last Monday when she arrived home from work. "Auntie Edith was livid. I have never seen her so mad."

"Was she mad at you?" BJ asked.

"Well, yes, with me, with Dad, with the world, it seemed," Emma explained. "Her doctor has told her she's heading for a breakdown and I'm part of the reason for that. I have to admit I have given her very little thought since you and I fell in love. I owe her an explanation really, don't you think?"

BJ looked at her with questioning eyes. "Did you tell her? Did you actually tell her about us?"

"No, of course not," she assured him. "I'm still lying through my teeth to her and I feel dreadful about that..."

"We are going to have to come clean sometime," BJ stated. "Why not now?"

"Because," Emma jumped in. "Because I'm still not sure how she will react. When I went to Jamaica, she hinted that she didn't..."

"Didn't what?"

"It's hard to say really. She didn't actually say she didn't like your people, but she intimated that she'd be wary of you all." She took his hand in hers. "Enough of that, though, because I have some really important news for you..."

Bang! Crash! A brick came flying through the window and broken glass spattered around the room.

"What the...?" BJ jumped up and looked through the broken window only to see two teenaged boys running down the street as though wild animals were after them. Turning back to Emma, he saw the shock in her eyes. "And now it begins," he said sadly. "I wish I could say it won't happen again, but I can't. I'm going to have to report it to the police, I'm afraid."

Emma bent to retrieve the note that was attached to the missile that had literally shattered their peace. *Go back to where you belong, nigger. We don't want you in Slough.*

~ * ~

BJ called the constabulary on the communal telephone in the entrance hall. He and Emma had said very little after the offending projectile had suddenly and immediately put paid to the joy of reconnecting after a few days of self-imposed isolation. "Perhaps you should leave before the police arrive," he suggested. "We don't want to be questioned about our relationship, especially by them. They'd want to question you and your home address would have to be given. That could open up a can of worms, couldn't it? I'll tell them I was alone, so you won't be involved..."

Emma went to hug him, reassurance for them both, but he moved away. "BJ, what's up?"

"Not now, Emma," he said. "Too much going on in my mind. You go now before they get here."

"You'd better move those cups then," she advised him. "Two cups, one with lipstick on the rim, will tell them a good story without you telling it yourself." She grabbed her coat and her handbag and left through the back door so as not to draw attention to herself.

BJ watched as she walked quickly away from the building. His thoughts were dark and threatening. *I have not seen nor heard that word for years. Mild abuse I am prepared to deal with, but the N word—I want to kill the perpetrators.*

"Mr Johnson?" the burly policeman called as he pushed open the door.

"Come in, sir," BJ said and as he hastily removed the cups from the table and into the sink, "Can I make you a cup of tea?

"Not just now, Mr Johnson. Now tell me what happened..."

Nineteen

Emma decided to stay at home over the weekend. On Saturday morning, her father was taken to his new residence, and he surprised both his daughter and his sister when he waved to them as the car pulled away. "My goodness," Edith remarked. "Is that a happy cheerio, or a final goodbye? I think I detected the hint of a smile on his lips."

"Who knows?" Emma said glumly. "We'll just have to interpret it as we see fit."

"My, my, Emma," her aunt commented. "Don't tell me you are sad to see him go. After all, it was you who first suggested the move for him. Are you having second thoughts?"

"Not at all," Emma told her. "I'm not feeling well at the moment and I need to go back to bed if you don't mind. I have to get better by Monday. I have so much work waiting for me..."

"But you did it last evening after school closed, didn't you?" Edith pointed out. *Let's hear your excuse now, young lady.*

"I did some, but I didn't finish it all," she lied again. "I really should get back into doing it all before I leave in the evening. Now that Dad's not here, there won't be as much urgency for me to rush home."

"Whatever you think, Emma. Whatever you think." Edith had plans of her own and wasn't about to divulge them to her niece.

Come Monday morning, Emma was still feeling sick and while she knew the reason why, she couldn't share her joy with anybody until she had informed BJ of his impending fatherhood. She pushed down a slice of toast for her breakfast and sipped a cup of tea in an effort not to give morning sickness signs to her aunt. "I'll be off now," she called to Edith.

Edith appeared at the top of the stairs. "Will you be late home tonight?" she asked.

"Probably," Emma replied. "I'll have to see how things go during the day. I'll play it by ear. Expect me when you see me."

"Okay, dear," Edith called. She smiled to herself. *I'll see you at four o'clock, young lady, but you won't see me. I intend to get to the bottom of your furtive movements.*

~ * ~

Edith left the house at three-fifty and drove towards the school, making sure she found a parking spot where she might wait undetected. When the bell rang at four o'clock, she waited until Emma left the building. Sure enough, at five past four, Emma skipped down the steps from the entrance and made her way to the station. Edith's brain was in overdrive. *Now why would she go to the station?* she questioned silently. *Where has she been recently that might involve going on a train? She went to Slough when she used my car to help her friend move to a new house. She could be going to that friend's house, but it's a mystery why she wouldn't tell me. Visiting a girlfriend is normal. Girlfriend? Hmm?* She grimaced as she pondered on the question. *I'll have to risk going to Slough. I'll get there before the train if I leave straight away and I'll wait at the station to see where she goes from there. With luck, I'll catch her out. That'll teach her not to lie to me.*

~ * ~

Emma smiled to herself as she left Slough station. She knew BJ would be home before her as he'd been to a meeting with the local education officer to report his progress with the immigrant children.

Edith was overjoyed to find her supposition had been correct and she kept a suitable distance behind Emma as she walked the half mile to Langley Road. *I won't follow her in straight away,* she thought. *I'll wait half an hour or so and let her get settled into doing whatever she does on these occasions.* She smiled. *I like playing detective. Maybe I can become a sleuth in my old age.* She took out a magazine from the glove compartment and flicked through the pages while keeping a close eye on the building into which Emma had disappeared.

Inside the apartment, BJ had the tea ready as usual. "How are you, darling?" he asked quietly.

"I'm good, BJ, but why the sad face? Is that why you are sitting in the gathering gloom?"

"I'm not sad, I'm just a little more thoughtful than usual," he explained. "And I like the half-light. It's calming somehow."

"How did the meeting go?" she asked as she removed her coat and threw it across the sofa.

"Oh, it was good, I think…"

"Then what are you thinking about?" she asked. "Something is clearly bothering you?"

BJ sighed. "I hate myself for it, but I'm still stewing over the note that came flying through the window on Friday. I know I shouldn't, but it was more offensive than anything I've had to endure since I arrived here…"

Emma took his hand. "I understand, darling, and I have the perfect remedy to cheer you up and put a smile on your face." She smiled lovingly at the man who had swept her off her feet when it was least expected, the guy whom she loved and who loved her. "I'm pregnant."

Silence.

"Well, say something, please," she urged. "Say something... anything." She felt the colour drain from her face and she grabbed hold of the table to steady herself.

BJ went to catch her and flicked on the light so he could see her more clearly. He held her at arms' length and looked into her eyes...

In the car park below, Edith Booth was suddenly made aware that a light had come on in a first-floor window. She could see Emma's blonde hair and...*Oh my dear god! Please tell me I'm seeing things.*

~ * ~

Inside the apartment, BJ had steered Emma to the sofa and allowed her to lie down. He covered her with her coat and went to sit at her feet. After a few minutes of silence, he asked, "How did we get to this point?"

Emma was stunned. "We had sex every day for weeks," she blurted. "Surely you know that's how babies are made?"

"Don't be sarcastic, Emma," he reproached. "Babies weren't on my agenda."

Emma stared at him in horror. "But we talked of being together for ever. Surely marriage and babies would be the natural progression in our relationship. I can't believe you aren't happy about it."

BJ shook his head and declared, his voice broken with emotion, "I'm shocked, confused, tormented and angry all at the same time."

"And there's no room for happiness in there?" Emma asked shakily.

"How can I be happy about it, Emma?" he snapped. "We haven't even been honest with anybody about being together. I am in a country that isn't yet ready to accept me for the person I am. I am trying to prove my worth in a job I have never done before I came here. I had planned to settle in this alien place against the odds, but this changes everything for me. I have so much to do and to prove before I am ready to settle down."

Emma was distraught. "This isn't just about you, BJ. You have just preached at me saying *I, I, I, me, me, me!* What do I have to glean from that? You've had your fun and now get on your bike, Emma? It took two to tango, my friend. Babies aren't conceived without an egg coming together with a sperm. I produced the egg and you…"

"Stop this, Emma," he said firmly. "This will get us nowhere."

Emma sat up and grabbed her coat. "No, it won't, but you aren't the one with a baby in your belly…"

BJ stood and, arms akimbo, he bristled. "And a mixed-race baby, Emma. Have you considered that? You weren't ready to be seen with me in public, nor were you ready to introduce me to your family." He paced the floor, his arms flailing as he walked. "Have you thought what sort of a life the child might have growing up in this god-forsaken place? I had a brick thrown through my window last Friday and was called *nigger*. Have you any idea what that does to a person like me? Can't you…?"

The realisation hit Emma as soon as she detected the determination in BJ's voice. "I don't know you anymore, BJ, but I've heard enough. That's it. Don't you worry about me. Just get on with your uncomfortable little life until you are ready to make your mark in this god-forsaken, as you say, and unsociable place you have an incongruously overwhelming desire to call home. I hope you are able to accept that it might never happen, but in spite of what you have said, I wish you well. Goodbye, BJ. It was nice knowing you."

~ * ~

When she arrived home, her aunt was sitting in the drawing room staring into space. As Emma walked in, her face stained and bloated by tears of heartbreak and hurt, Edith looked at her with accusing eyes. "So you stayed late at school, did you?" she spat sarcastically. "You managed to get all that outstanding work done, did you?"

Emma flopped down in her dad's chair and didn't answer.

"I saw you, young lady. I saw you in the arms of a…"

Emma dared to smile wryly. "Turned detective, have you? That makes you just as bad as I am then, sneaking around behind my back. And you can say what you were going to say, Auntie. You saw me in the arms of a black man. And you know what? I don't care what you think. I'm not ashamed."

Edith was astonished. "My god, Emma. You ought to be more than ashamed. You have become a liar and a...and a..."

"A hussy? Is that what you want to say, Auntie?"

"Exactly. A hussy, a tart, a trollop...whatever you want to call yourself. I knew you must have been getting up to no good considering you were so secretive about your whereabouts and your friends. No wonder you didn't want to bring him home."

"Well, no need for you to bother further," Emma said wearily. "It's over. I'm pregnant and he doesn't want to know..."

"You are what?" Edith exclaimed.

"You heard me, Auntie. I'm pregnant, and I don't care that you disapprove. I'll have this baby, and I'll bring it up to be *loving* and *tolerant* and *accepting* of people for whom they are. This child will learn that bigotry and prejudice are only brandished around by ignorant people who really don't belong in the human race. I'll be gone by the end of the week."

Twenty

Birmingham, England – 1970

A group of university students gathered in the coffee bar in the students' union building. "Who can afford to go and see *Three Sisters* at the ABC? I have an assignment to do and Mrs Hough says the film will give clarity to the major themes in the story," Alison said. "Come on, who's up for it?"

Nobody offered to accompany her. "I can't afford another cup of coffee until my cheque clears," Daniel told her. "My mom was late mailing my money this month so that counts me out. Sorry."

"No worries," Alison conceded. "I'll go on my own."

"Take a knitting needle with you in case some sleazebag fondles your knee in the dark!" one guy joked.

They all laughed.

"Don't say that, T. I need to get every scrap of help I can for this essay," Alison admitted. "Jane?" she pleaded.

Jane shrugged.

"Oh please, Jane. What if I go halves with you for the ticket?"

"Deal, although Chekhov isn't really my cup of tea," Jane reluctantly agreed. "We'll have to go tonight though, 'cos I have tutorials all day tomorrow."

The seven students were a motley crew who had met up on the first day of the first term and, two years later, they were still together as study buddies and close friends. Alison Macdonald, a Scot from Edinburgh studying English and Russian Literature; Tommy Sheeran from County Clare, Ireland, studying hard to gain a degree in medical science; Alexa Papadakis, half-English, half-Greek, from Athens studying architecture; Lenny Bolton from Blackburn in Lancashire also studying architecture; Jane Smith-Jackson from London, doing a Post Graduate Certificate of Education after gaining a degree in modern languages; David Ashton, a local boy from Edgbaston, studying Law, and Daniel Williams, a half-Jamaican twenty-year-old studying Politics and Social Sciences.

Whilst they were in different faculties, apart from Alexa and Lenny who were both studying the same subject, they all lived in the same student Halls accommodation and socialised as often as they were able, work permitting.

Alison and Daniel were sitting in the common room one day when the others were in lectures. It wasn't often they were able to relax a bit and forget their studies for a while, but this day both had completed their assignments in good time and sat listening to the music blaring forth from Radio Caroline.

"Hey, man," Daniel called amicably across the room. "You know the government doesn't allow Caroline. It'll be blocked soon. Put Radio One on, please."

The guy laughed. "I'm not bothered and neither should you be. This reggae should take you back to your roots."

"Why do you say that?" Alison asked, her hackles rising immediately.

"He's black, isn't he? All black men like reggae. They invented it."

Daniel remained silent.

"Don't you think you are generalising, not to mention the personal nature of your remarks...?"

Daniel caught Alison's arm. "Don't, Ali. It's okay. Don't make a scene."

"But why don't you stand up for yourself?" she asked in a dramatic whisper. "He seems to have a problem—"

"Then it's his problem, not mine," Daniel assured her.

The guy walked towards them and taunted Daniel. "Come on, Rasta, show us your moves." And he started jumping around like a chimpanzee, scratching his armpits and making monkey noises that were offensive and grossly insulting.

"Daniel!" Alison cried. "Don't let him treat you like that." Then to the ignoramus who laughed at his own performance, "Go back to swinging from tree to tree, you imbecile. You're impressing nobody here."

The guy rudely looked around the room for acknowledgement. All heads were down, pointedly ignoring his extremely insensitive, impolite, unsociable antics.

"Show some humility, you ignorant bas..."

"Don't, Alison. Don't lower your own standards for him. He's not worth it," Daniel said calmly.

The guy looked around the room again and still gained no response. He shrugged and to everybody's surprise, actually blushed shamefacedly as he walked away.

"Good riddance." Alison couldn't resist having the last word. She had been incensed for Daniel. "Why did you let him carry on like that? You would have been within your rights to smack him in the face. I know I was ready to do just that."

"I have been brought up to be tolerant of such people. I've told you before, my mother is a white English woman and my father is... was...a black Jamaican."

"I know you've told us, but I didn't know you had lost your father. I'm sorry, Dan." Alison apologised.

"Don't be sorry. I haven't lost him. He's not dead." His guard was up. I haven't told them my father is a famous writer. I'd prefer to keep that to myself. "He's had nothing to do with my upbringing. My mom left England because of such prejudice and ignorance. Some of it on his part in an introverted or introspective sort of way. She has a house in Kingston and that's where I lived for eighteen years. Coming here to study was preferred by me and with my mom's approval. We both thought I might see for myself the narrow-mindedness and the racial prejudice that still exists, even in this day and age. When you think about it, black doctors, athletes and the like are helping Britain to maintain the social and economic standards the government and the population expect. It's all difficult to understand for somebody like me. I'm really not black, but brown, rather like those Brits who spend two weeks annually in Spain or Greece, desperate to get a tan and look like me." He laughed. "Don't worry about that guy, Ali. There'll always be people like him and I'm fine, honestly."

"But it's going on everywhere," Alison continued, getting on her horse that was growing higher and higher by the second. "Look at football crowds. There are hooligans who go to matches especially to harass the black players and yet, those brilliant, black footballers are the people keeping their teams on top of the league. And there are black athletes all over the world. How can you just ignore it? It's only a couple of years ago there was a scandal with the English cricket board choosing Basil D'Oliveira, a coloured South African immigrant, to play against his native land. The apartheid laws in South Africa are disgusting. The Test series was cancelled because the South African government wouldn't allow him to play at their cricket grounds. It makes my blood boil."

"Don't worry about it, Ali. You can't single-handedly change the world," Daniel told her calmly. "People like you and me and my mom can quietly go about our business in our own way and hope that our humility will rub off on those who are in a position to make a difference, but in all honesty, there will always be the ignorant ones who treat other races with disrespect. It happens in Jamaica, too, but not quite as bad as it is here. In the meantime, we just have to get on with our lives without rustling feathers."

~ * ~

At the end of the final term that year, Daniel decided not to fly home for the summer break. "I'll get a holiday job and hopefully stay in Halls over the summer."

"Don't stay here on your own, Dan," the local boy, David, said. "You can stay at mine, but won't your mom want you home?"

"I went home at Christmas and I told her then that I might not go back in the summer…"

"You must be mad," Lenny interrupted. "You mean to say you prefer the British summer cold and rain to the Jamaican sunshine? I know where I'd be spending the summer if I lived in a hot climate."

Daniel grinned, a warm dazzling smile that somehow always captured the group's attention and they all smiled with him. "That's just it, Len. I have lived there all my life, so I know it will still be there if, and when, I go back after I'm qualified. Anyway, a change is as good as a rest, so they say."

"Well, what about staying with me?" David asked again.

Daniel pursed his lips and sucked in a deep breath. "No offence, Dave, but I think I'd rather stay here. I want to come and go as I please and I would feel obliged to stick around your place out of respect for you and your family. The university gives overseas students the option of staying on campus during the summer. Being here and hopefully earning money during the day will give me the freedom I would like. Sorry if I sound ungrateful."

"Not a problem," David assured him. "You can always come over to Edgbaston when the cricket's on. It's the England and West Indies Test in August."

"Sounds great," Daniel said. "Thanks."

Twenty-one

Daniel secured a bartender's job at the Black Swan hotel, within walking distance of the university. His shifts varied; some were morning until late afternoon; others evenings from six o'clock until midnight. Some days when he was working the late shift, he went to the library, not really to study, although he did have university work to do before term started again in September. He decided he might do some lighter reading and was able to sit on the balcony when the weather was occasionally warm enough to be outdoors. Wandering round the library shelves one day, he happened upon a novel entitled *Where Black Men Dare* by BJ Johnson. He stopped abruptly. He knew who his father was, but had not read any of his books, even though his works were renowned not only for the interesting and intriguing storylines, but also for the author's reflections and social commentary on being a black man living in twentieth century Britain. He cast his eyes along the shelf where there were numerous books by the same author: *Angels Don't Have Black Faces, Follow Your*

Dreams, Love Does Not Conquer All were a few of the titles, but the one that intrigued him most was entitled *Belonging*.

Daniel turned the book over in his hands before he opened it to read the blurb on the back cover: *Margaret, a secretary, meets William, a teacher, at work in a city not ready to accept racial differences. She is a white woman; he is a black man. While illicit love blossoms, they try to find a way to be together without incurring the wrath of not only family and friends, but also of the world in general. Will their love be strong enough to lead them to happiness or will powerful outside influences force them apart?* He flipped through the pages to the back where the author's biographical notes were and wandered over to an empty table. He made himself comfortable. There was a photograph of the author and Daniel stared at his smile, a smile he had seen daily in a mirror. His own features strongly resembled those of the man in the photo, apart from a hint of silver at the author's temples. He felt an overpowering compulsion to read on. *BJ Johnson came to England to work in 1948. A former war correspondent and journalist in his native Jamaica, he trained as a teacher in London and taught English and multi-cultural studies until 1965 when he retired from teaching to take up his love of writing full time. Most of his work, whilst fiction, is based on his life experiences living amongst people who, in his opinion, were not ready to accept those of a different culture.*

Daniel closed his eyes and placed his head in his hands. *Mom didn't tell me details of their relationship, just that they were very much in love. When it came to the crunch, this man didn't have the guts to face the problems head-on as far as I can gather. My interpretation of his bio is that he didn't feel at home here and yet, he has stayed for almost twenty years. Nor has he kept in touch with my mother and doesn't know he has a son. Hmm, I wonder why.*

~ * ~

"But why on earth are you reading his books now?" Emma asked during their weekly telephone call.

"Sudden interest, I guess," Daniel said. "My social sciences tutor is often quoting from his work to illustrate the nature of British society today. Have you read any of them, Mom?"

"No...but I *have* been tempted, I must admit," Emma told him. "I think my stubborn streak won't allow me to contribute to his income by buying his books." She laughed, a sort of nervous laugh that Daniel detected was covering up her true feelings.

"Do you mind if I read them?" he asked tentatively. "I would like to find out his views and it would be ironic if he helped me get a first class degree, wouldn't it?"

Emma was quiet and then spoke with a hint of uncertainty in her voice. "If you must, Danny boy. In all honesty, reading what he has written might take me to places I would prefer not to be."

"What do you mean?" Daniel interrupted. "When you call me Danny boy, I know you are sad. I thought your love for him was strong at the time."

"At the time, yes, it was, but not strong enough, it seems."

"But will it upset you if I try to get into his mind through his writing?" Daniel asked quietly.

Emma breathed in deeply. "No, I won't be upset, but please don't ask me to discuss what he has written, because that would probably put me in situations I am trying to forget, even twenty years on."

"I promise I won't involve you," Daniel assured her, but his thoughts were speculative. *Poor Mom. She must have felt she was living in a nightmare and every time she looks at me, she must see him. Even I can see the likeness.*

"I'll go now, Daniel. Take care. I love you, baby."

"I love you too, Mom," he confirmed. "Always and for ever. Speak next week. Bye."

~ * ~

The summer holidays flew past and Daniel was pleased to see the old crowd back together again, apart from Jane, who had qualified and was taking up her first teaching post in a posh London school.

"Did you miss me?" Alison asked him, throwing her arms around him and giving him a friendly, Scottish hug.

"Of course I did, but I missed your role as my personal bodyguard more. I had to tell several inebriated guys in the Black Swan to back off a few times. I think you would have been in your element defending my honour!"

Alison punched him in the ribs playfully. "Away with you," she said in her broadest Scottish accent, and then she hugged the others in turn to welcome them back.

"I caught up with Daniel for the Test match at Edgbaston," David told them. "He didn't know who to support and he couldn't lose really. His English half was successful this time, but I think the Caribbean half of him will be cheering his team on for a few years to come. The potential in their team is definitely something to watch out for."

They all laughed and Daniel quipped, "All in your mind, Dave. I'm not into cricket really, but I enjoyed the match and I can boast about having seen Gary Sobers and Clive Lloyd in the flesh. I'll be the envy of my uncles Earl and Leroy. They love their cricket." Then he changed the subject. "Look at you, Lenny. Where have you been to get such a brilliant tan?"

Lenny had stood quietly with Alexa while all the cricket talk was going on. When Daniel asked the question, he placed his arm around Alexa's shoulders and announced, "I decided after a week at home that I'd go to Athens...to study the architecture firsthand..."

"Is that all?" Alison asked as she observed the closeness of her friends.

"Well, not quite all," Alexa said coyly. "Lenny and I are—"

"An item?" Alison interrupted excitedly.

"Yes we are," Lenny announced. "Hope you guys are comfortable with that."

There were loud answers ringing around the room of, *"Of course we are! Love is in the air! But don't be hanging onto each other all the time, please!"*

"We won't make you feel you are in the way, promise," Lenny said light-heartedly. "We have finals like the rest of you this year so work is our priority."

Two days later, lectures began in full force. Timetables were full, assignments were many and their free time diminished.

When Christmas was approaching, they were all looking forward to a welcome break, but there was work to be done before they might relax. Daniel arrived at the lecture hall for the final session with his social sciences tutor. Members of all years had been told it would be advantageous to attend this particular lecture, so it would be silly to skip it as some were disposed to do on occasions. Hence the lecture hall was full of sociology students from first, second, and third years, and Daniel squeezed along the back row to find a vacant seat.

Professor Lingard strode to his lectern in the centre of the platform. "Welcome, sociology students. *I* am *not* going to speak to you today..."

There was a general gasp around the room, some of surprise, some of confusion, some of amusement.

"...other than to introduce to you our guest speaker. We are very privileged and honoured that he has given up some of his valuable time to be with us. Please give a warm Birmingham university welcome to Mr BJ Johnson..."

Daniel felt his heart skip a beat.

Twenty-two

Daniel hung on every word BJ Johnson was saying. His mind was in overdrive and he had to stop himself trying to fit his mother into what was being said. Personal relationships were not mentioned at all and he was disappointed that it seemed his mom had not affected BJ Johnson's life in some way. *Surely, Mom must have played a part in his attitudes to life in general. He is just talking about public persona really...their opinions of him, his opinions of them and how he had to make bold efforts to hang onto his self-worth. Maybe personal connections form another part of his lectures, separate from generalisations of public opinion. On the other hand, he might think his personal life has nothing to do with a bunch of wet-behind-the-ears students.* He looked directly at the man behind the lectern. *I must clear my mind of my connection to this man if I want to benefit in any way from his experiences.*

The speaker continued. "Last and, by no means least, I might just mention my experiences as a correspondent at the end of the last war. I was sent to report on what was happening at Bergen-Belsen.

Psychologically, I didn't cope well with what I saw, but later when I had time to think it through, I realised that those people who were in the prison camp were suffering from prejudice on a scale much, much larger than I ever would. I felt shame, for a while, that I was being self-centred and patronising to all those who suffered at the hands of people who condemned them just for being whom they are. In spite of my own feelings about racial prejudice, I was, and I *am* humbled by them. If you read my book, *The Devil's Hand,* it explains how I felt then, how I feel now and how it will affect me for the rest of my life. Thank you for listening and good luck to you all."

Tumultuous applause echoed round the room and students stood in appreciation of BJ Johnson who had enlightened them on dealing with the age-old social problems that never seem to go away. Daniel remained seated, uncertain of what he ought to do. Nobody noticed as he sneaked out as the thunderous applause continued. He waited until most of the students had left the building, but a few stood by hoping to catch another glimpse of the renowned author before he left. When he appeared at the door, they rushed forward to ask for autographs on their sociology files.

Daniel stayed behind them, leaning on the wall with his hands in his pockets. When the others dispersed, he remained there just observing the man who was his father. BJ looked at him, paused just for a moment, nodded in Daniel's direction, and went on his way.

~ * ~

Emma welcomed her son home for Christmas. "It seems ages since I saw you," she told him as she met him at the airport. "You look tired, son."

Daniel gave her a hug. "I've been travelling for fifteen hours and flying for ten of those," he said with a wry smile. "I'm tired and jet-lagged. I need my bed right now, but I do appreciate your buying the ticket. I couldn't be here without the advantage of the direct flights from London. Thank you. You're a legend!"

"That's enough of the bull," Emma said with a smile. "I'm just so glad you are able to spend Christmas with us. We're going to Auntie

Ann's for Christmas dinner and then they are all coming to us on Boxing Day."

"Sounds good," Daniel replied. "How are Glory and Teddy? It'll be good to catch up with them."

"Some news there," Emma told him. "I told you when we spoke on the phone that Glory is engaged to Leroy's nephew, Tyson. Well, they plan to get married next year when they've saved up the deposit for a house. Teddy has suddenly decided he's going to New York after Christmas. Ann and Earl are quite upset. There's a lot of talk about the Black Liberation Army and knowing what a hot-head Teddy is, none of us can be sure what he'll do when he gets there."

"Sounds bad," Daniel said. "I know he's older than me, but I'll see what I can find out from him. We get along well, and he might talk to me rather than to his parents."

"That'd be great, Dan. Now let's get you home and to bed."

He woke to the sound of his mother crying. Racing downstairs, he saw Emma on her knees weeping into her hands. "What on earth's the matter, Mom?"

Emma was sobbing pitifully. "My dad," she cried. "He passed away...he died suddenly without ever speaking to me. In over twenty years, he didn't try to contact me."

Daniel knelt beside her and took her in his arms. "I don't know what to say, Mom. From what I can gather, he probably didn't even remember you as his daughter. Dementia is a horrible illness and especially so when it was apparently brought on through trauma. Just try to think of all the good times before he went to war. I gather he was never the same person when he returned."

"But one word of caring would have sufficed," she wailed. "Why couldn't he just say one kind word to me?"

"How did you find out?" he asked.

"The Willows' matron-in-charge sent me a letter," Emma said, a little calmer then. "I wrote to Dad about six months ago and one of the nurses apparently read my letter to him at the time. I don't know what his reaction was, but he obviously didn't intimate to her that he wanted to reply. This is such a shock and just before Christmas too."

"I wonder why your aunt didn't let you know."

Emma sniffed. "Oh, *she* wouldn't let me know. She disowned me when I got pregnant with you. I can't be sure if she went to see Dad regularly. She was on the verge of a breakdown at that time and, even though I did send her cards on her birthdays and Christmases every year since I left, she never acknowledged them and didn't send any cards to me on any occasion. She could also have died and I would never know. Dad was seventy so she must be seventy-five if she's still with us."

"I guess we've managed so far without them and we'll carry on doing our own thing, but I'm sad for you and, also, that I'll never meet my grandfather…"

"I wouldn't want you to see him as he was, Danny boy. I'm very sad he's gone, but I feel I lost him a long time ago."

They sat in each other's arms for a while, each with their own thoughts until Emma stirred and said, "Come on, son. We have preparations to make for Boxing Day. I thought we'd have a barbecue to keep it simple. What do you think?"

"Sounds good, Mom," he said. "I'll be head chef!"

~ * ~

Christmas and New Year came and went without any further dramas. A couple of days before Teddy was due to leave for New York, Daniel invited him out for a beer. "It seems your mom and dad aren't too sure about you going to New York," he said pointedly. "What's the story, Ted?"

"No story, man," Teddy replied. "I'm going to see my girl—"

"And that's no story?" Daniel interrupted.

"Not for me," Teddy said. "But if I tell my folks why I'm going, they'll make a big story out of it and I don't want that."

"But you could give them some sort of explanation, surely."

"I have," Teddy pointed out. "I've told them I'm going for work, which is true. I can't be working for my dad forever. Every time I say I want to leave his mechanics business, he goes mad, man! He tells me it's my inheritance and I should be pleased to work for him. I want more experience than just working on second-hand vehicles and souped-up motor bikes. I need to work on Chevies and Mustangs and Dodges, not to mention the BMWs that are gaining ground in the US market just now."

"Have you explained that to him?" Daniel asked. "My mom says they think you might get yourself mixed up with the Black Liberation Army. There was some pretty bad press about the Black Panthers last October. I even read about it in England."

"They've said that to me too, and there's nothing further from my mind," Teddy explained. "I know I'm a hot-head at times, especially when Mom treats me like a kid. I always go off on a rant then, but I'm a pacifist at heart. I'm not looking for trouble. I just want to be with my girl."

"Then tell them."

"Then I'll get the lecture about sex before marriage, birth control and my responsibilities and respect for girls. I mean, I'm twenty-five years old, Dan!" Teddy sighed deeply. "They first started on about that years ago when I took my first girl to the school prom. I lost my temper because I know they had sex before they were married and Glory was the result, so I told them they'd no room to talk and they were hypocrites. That almost started world war three, so I decided not mention Eliza to them. It's easier for me if I just tell them I'm going to broaden my experience. Even then, I get the third degree." He shrugged and grinned. "How about you, Dan?"

"All good for me," he said cheerfully. "I have *girl* friends, but not a girlfriend. Our group of six—used to be seven, but one qualified and left uni—are like a family and we look out for each other all the time. I like Alison, one of the girls, and I think she likes me, but we haven't taken it further."

"Do you want to?"

"Not at the moment, but who knows what will happen once we qualify?" Daniel said.

"What *will* happen when you finish your studies?" Teddy asked. "Are you coming home to work?"

"That depends," Daniel told him.

"On what?"

Daniel looked pensive.

"Come on, my little buddy. What gives?" Teddy urged.

"Basically, it will be whether I can get a job here in the field of my studies. I really want to work with immigrants...West Indians, Asians, meaning Indians, Pakistanis and Chinese as well as Eastern Europeans who are having difficulties settling in a new country, and I'm sure there will be more work for me in Britain than there would be here in Jamaica." He paused poignantly. "I might even get into politics; then I could really make a difference."

"So, what's bothering you, Dan?" Teddy asked. "I can see you have something on your mind."

Daniel looked at his feet before he spoke then looking directly at Teddy he said, "I saw my dad."

"Oh lordy, lordy! You actually saw him and spoke to him?"

"No, I didn't speak to him. He was giving a lecture at the end of the semester. He was interesting, very interesting, but it was hard not to think of him and Mom together all the time he was speaking. After the lecture, I waited to see him with a few other students. I didn't approach him when *they* did, but when they went away, I stayed leaning against a wall watching him."

"Oh lordy, lordy," Teddy said again. "Did he see you?"

Daniel shifted in his seat. "Well, yes and it might be in my imagination, but I think he was taken aback, because he stopped briefly, then nodded to me as he left."

"Does your mom know about this?" Teddy asked, curiosity urging him on.

"No!" Daniel stated firmly. "I can't tell her, as she'll only worry when I go back next week. She can't even read his books because she says they will take her into situations she'd rather forget."

"So what is worrying *you*, Dan?" Teddy asked sympathetically.

"I think I want to meet him," he admitted. "Part of me wants him to know I'm his son, and part of me wants him to see I made it without him. I also want to punch him in the mouth for leaving my mom to raise me on her own."

Teddy patted him on the shoulder. "It's a difficult one, Dan, but I won't say anything about it to anybody. You have my word," he assured Daniel. "We both have a secret that we need to keep for each other. I'm so glad we spoke about them tonight. A problem shared and all that."

"Thanks, Ted. You have my word, too."

Twenty-three

Daniel arrived back in Birmingham, England during the first week in January 1971. He was, as usual, the first back in Halls and he was surprised when the bursar called him down to the phone. "Hello?" he said tentatively.

"It's Mom, Daniel. I've just had a letter from a solicitor in London," she told him. "Guess what!"

"What?" Daniel said. "How can I guess what's in a letter from a solicitor. Have you broken the law and been subpoenaed?"

Emma breathed in audibly. "Don't be silly. My dad made a will before he went overseas, and nobody knew about it until the authorities were informed of his death. Everything was supposed to go to Mum, but I'm the next of kin and so it now comes to me. He had all his savings in a high interest account, and it seems I am due a cheque for—wait for it—twenty thousand pounds! I can't believe it."

Daniel did a quick calculation in his head. "That's about forty thousand in Jamaican dollars! Lordy, lordy, Mom, we're rich!"

"I wouldn't say we're rich, but it will certainly make things easier. I could cut back on my hours at school, but I love my job and it keeps me occupied, especially when you're away. I'm an expert on the Xerox machine now. I have learned so much since my job at Windsor Primary School."

Daniel went quiet. *I don't want this conversation about what I'll be doing next year.* He coughed to recover his equilibrium. "That's up to you, Mom," he said. "I don't think you are old enough to retire. I'd invest the money and let it work for you."

"How sensible," Emma said proudly. "I'll go now, but I just wanted to tell you of our good fortune. Work hard at your studies and I shall now be able to consider going over there for your degree ceremony. That will be some homecoming after twenty-one years, won't it? Bye, darling. Love you."

"Love you too, Mom. Bye."

~ * ~

With everybody back on campus by the middle of January, lectures began in earnest and Daniel threw himself into completing his dissertation entitled, *American and British Racial and Ethnic Politics 1834 to 1970*. He had a private tutorial with his professor every Wednesday morning and, although his field of study was ambitious, between them they felt it would give Daniel plenty of research and, ultimately, knowledge for working both in Britain and the United States after qualification.

Aside from his studies, he was talking to Alison one morning when he felt the need to share his intentions regarding his father. "I didn't say anything before, because he wasn't a part of my life, but when he came here at the end of last term, he became an entity, somebody who actually exists whom I need to know. Previously he was only an imagined character because I'd never met him. Now I can literally picture him in my head. I couldn't do that before."

Alison grabbed his hand. "Gosh, Dan, you certainly kept all that quiet. Fancy BJ Johnson being your father! I can't believe it."

"I needed to tell somebody here. I need a sounding board. It can't be broadcast, Ali. It would have too many repercussions if anybody on the course knew about it. Can you imagine how everybody would presume my views are the same as his? I could be regarded as his puppet…"

"Hold on, Dan," Alison interrupted. "Aren't you becoming presumptive yourself?"

"How do you mean?"

"Well, how can you say what others might think?" she asked pointedly. "They might not even care that you're BJ Johnson's son."

"Sorry, Ali. That must have sounded really conceited."

"No, it didn't," she assured him. "I know you and being an egotist is not your style. What does your mum think?"

"I haven't told her."

"Blimey! Why not?"

"Because she would flip! She can't even read his books for fear of being reminded of the time she was with him. Between you and me, I don't think she has ever stopped loving him, although she would never admit it. In all my life, I have never heard her bad-mouth him except to say he didn't have the balls to face public scrutiny in a mixed relationship."

"That's sad," Alison said quietly. "Do you think she would object to you making this decision without consulting her?"

"Probably, but I don't want to have more of a conscience about it than I have now. If she knew, I'm sure she would try to stop me contacting him."

"Then why incur the wrath of the woman who has cared for you and nurtured you all your life?" Alison asked.

Daniel sighed. "I know what you're saying, Ali, but I don't think, if she really thought about it, she would deny me the chance of knowing my father. I genuinely believe that." He looked down and noticed Alison was still holding his hand. He grinned. "Are you being my surrogate mother, Ali?"

Alison released his hand immediately, and blushing slightly, she said, "In your dreams, Williams!"

~ * ~

Having released some of the tension during his chat with Alison, Daniel completed his assignments with renewed vigour. Lectures stopped halfway through the term to allow dissertations to be completed and revision for exams to be done. In quiet moments, he thought about how he might contact his father. *Should I write to him first or should I just turn up at his home? I guess the former is best. I would hate to travel to...don't be stupid, Daniel. How do you know where he lives? You'd have to write to the publishers and ask if they might forward your letter.* So he wrote and put his trust in Shining Light Publishers to pass on the letter to BJ Johnson.

Weeks passed without any acknowledgement at all, then one Saturday morning, Daniel was called to Admin. When he arrived, Professor Lingard was there. "Good morning, Daniel. There is somebody here I would like you to meet."

Twenty-four

"This is Charles Winters from Shining Light Publishers."

"How do you do, sir," Daniel said as he offered a firm handshake to the gentleman in front of him.

"I am well, thank you, and you?" Winters replied.

"Good, thank you, sir."

"Do you know why I am here?" the gentleman asked.

Daniel took in a deep breath. "I think so. It possibly has something to do with the letter I wrote to BJ Johnson," he said. "I can think of no other reason why a publisher would want to see me."

"Do you mind talking in front of Professor Lingard?"

"Not at all," Daniel assured him. "Professor Lingard is my personal tutor and mentor..."

"And I'm wondering why I knew nothing of this before, young man," the professor said, smiling at his mentee.

Daniel felt his cheeks burning. "I'm sorry, Prof. I haven't spoken to anybody about it, apart from a close friend in Jamaica and Alison MacDonald who is in my peer group. It was only after I attended Mr

Johnson's lecture that I felt the need to contact him. He has never been a part of my life. There is no animosity attached to it and no hidden agenda. My letter was very vague, I know, but I didn't want Mr Johnson to react negatively to my suggestion that we meet. Now I am wondering if he wants to see me at all, considering Mr Winters has come in his place. I really didn't intend for him to travel to Birmingham from…"

"From where?" Winters asked.

Daniel was taken aback. He shrugged. "I don't know. I think he used to live in Slough, but he may have moved on. That's why I wrote to Shining Light."

"Is your mother aware of what you are suggesting?"

"No, sir, she is not. She would worry if she knew and I didn't know whether it would happen anyway. I would tell her after the event, of course, that is, *if* it should happen."

There was a moment of silence and Daniel looked first at his mentor and then at Charles Winters, who was the first to speak. "BJ is on a lecture tour for the next couple of weeks, but he says he would like to meet you when he returns from Scotland. He lives just outside Stratford-Upon-Avon, so not too far away from Birmingham. He will reply to your letter to arrange a meeting."

Daniel's face lit up with excitement. "I'll look forward to that. Thank you so much."

"My pleasure," Winters told him. "And for the record, you are the image of him!"

~ * ~

Exactly two weeks later, Daniel received an invitation to meet BJ Johnson at The Midland hotel at ten-thirty on Saturday morning… *'providing you have a little time to spare in the midst of revising for your exams.'* He told Alison about it, but nobody else. "I'm excited and nervous both at the same time. It could go one of two ways. It might all be wonderful and make me feel exhilarated before my first paper, or it could all go pear-shaped and leave me feeling that I don't have the incentive to take the exams at all."

"Don't be daft, Dan," Alison scolded. "I wish I could be a fly on the wall, but I think this is something you must face alone, dear friend."

"So it is," Daniel agreed. "But if I could take a friend, it would be you, Ali. Thanks for being there for me."

Taking his hand, Alison smiled affectionately. "Always, Dan, always."

~ * ~

Dressing casually in bell-bottomed jeans and a light grey cashmere sweater, Daniel, with butterflies marauding inside his belly, arrived at The Midland Hotel five minutes early. BJ was already there, sitting in a private alcove just off the reception area. As Daniel walked in, he stood and moved forward to greet him. "Good morning," he said quietly. "How are you?"

"I'm well, sir," Daniel replied confidently. "Thank you so much for agreeing to see me."

BJ signalled to Daniel to take a seat and then sat opposite him. "We met previously, didn't we?"

"I don't think so, sir."

"After my gig at the university. Weren't you leaning on the wall as I left?"

"Ah, then you did notice me. I wasn't sure if I had imagined that you looked in my direction," Daniel said somewhat shyly. "I didn't want to draw attention to myself at that juncture. The whole situation of your being there in the flesh was really a shock to the system."

"Oh, my lord, am I so formidable?" BJ asked, nervousness showing in his laugh.

Daniel smiled back at him. "I have to ask," he dared to say and getting right to the point, "You do know why I needed to meet you, don't you?"

BJ looked directly at him. "Of course I do and I wondered if you were going to punch me in the face for what I have done, or more to the point, what I have not done."

"I thought about it," Daniel admitted, not trying to hide his grin. "But I realised I needed to see where I had come from, how I evolved, if you understand what I mean."

"I do," BJ agreed. "I see a lot of your mother in your manner... confident and articulate, but without the..." He paused. "...without the bossiness I often accused her of in the early days."

Daniel smiled again. "I've been victim of that on numerous occasions, but she always capitulates in the end."

"Indeed she does...did," BJ agreed. "Is she aware of this meeting?"

"No," Daniel said firmly.

BJ looked sad. "Am I off limits? I wouldn't blame her or you if you have hated me for the past twenty years."

Daniel thought for a few moments about what he should say. "Hate is a strong word and I would hesitate to use it in this situation. She never shied away from telling me who my father was, but she didn't share her feelings, good or bad, about you. Only when I grew old enough to ask questions did she tell me that she would prefer not to revisit the past. I assumed it was too painful for her, but she never said so. She did make a clear request that I shouldn't ask questions about you. It was only when I came across your books in the library that I became more curious."

"Did Emma know about that?" BJ asked.

"She did and she said she didn't mind if I read the books, but I was warned not to try and discuss them with her," Daniel told him honestly. "Can I be blunt?"

"Of course. I wouldn't expect anything less."

"Why didn't you ever try to make contact in the past twenty years?" he asked. "You knew mom was pregnant when she left..."

"That was just it, she left and I didn't blame her. My attitude was vindictive, selfish, abominable, uncaring, however you choose to describe it. I did try to contact her through the school where we worked, but they didn't seem to have the information I was seeking. I went to her aunt's house and was bombarded with a torrent of abuse. I expected that, because I suspected Emma had been treated in a similar manner. Hence, I had no idea where she had gone." He looked directly at Daniel. "Do you still live in London?"

"Lordy, lordy!" Daniel exclaimed. "No! I was born in Kingston."

BJ looked wide-eyed at his son and shook his head at the sudden realisation. "I should have known," he said. "I knew she had a house in uptown Kingston and it didn't enter my head she would go there. It seemed logical for her to lose herself in London somewhere and I always hoped her aunt would look after her after the initial shock. What a fool I am. I should have thought it through when my brain was not consumed with—"

"Guilt?" Daniel boldly interrupted.

BJ looked sad. "I can't even hold guilt as a factor, I'm afraid. Whatever I say at this point will appear selfish and totally inexpedient, but the fact of the matter is, at the time I had been shocked by a flying brick coming through my window forcing me to think I could never belong in England, not how I wanted to belong. In an instant, I saw Emma getting pregnant as interfering with the bonding process. Neither of us had had the courage to go public with our relationship for fear of the consequences."

"What do you mean by bonding?"

"I needed to bond with the country and its people," BJ explained. "I saw no way of doing that if I had done something which wasn't then acceptable in the society I had chosen to live. In my eyes, a mixed-race child would suffer socially because I was selfish enough to impregnate a white woman. I personally had offended that society by falling in love." He covered his face with his hands.

Daniel reached across and touched his arm. "I think I understand your reasoning, but those were human lives you were dealing with."

"I know, I know, and I'm so sorry. Hindsight is a wonderful thing and I have often thought how Emma would have coped. She was a strong woman with strong views and..."

Daniel waited for him to complete the sentence, but BJ seemed to crumble under the strain. "My mother is all of those things, but she has a kind heart. She doesn't judge anybody at face value, regardless of the colour of their skin. She lives in what has now become quite a multi-cultural society in Jamaica. Many of her close friends are black, some brown like me and some whose skins are neither white nor brown, more olive. We live amongst them and although we are aware of prejudices outside our circle of friends, we don't court antagonism."

"Can you ever forgive me, Daniel?" BJ asked. "I know I don't deserve it, but I would so like to be a part of your life and try to make up for what I have missed."

"Did you ever marry and have other children?" Daniel inquired. "Do I have brothers or sisters?"

BJ shook his head. "I only ever loved once."

Both men stood and hugged like father and son.

"We can try, Dad; we can try."

Twenty-five

Daniel threw himself into exam preparation, but managed to meet BJ for lunch every other Saturday. Their conversations were always light and cheerful. Daniel couldn't help but tease a little on occasions. "We are bonding," he said frequently.

"So we are," BJ would respond. "Do you reckon we are succeeding?"

"Well," Daniel would say, "We are still a black man and a brown boy living in a predominantly white society, but I reckon we've come a long way since nineteen-fifty."

"Indeed, we have, son, indeed we have," BJ would reply, always quietly, but with so much emotion in his voice. "Have you told Emma yet that we are *bonding,* as we say?"

"Not yet," Daniel admitted. "I need to be able to approach my exams with my mind focussed on my subjects. If I tell her now, I cannot guarantee that she would react calmly, especially if she knew we had been doing all this behind her back for weeks. She has hated secrecy ever since her own...and your...clandestine activities. That is the only thing she has admitted about your relationship. She has so many regrets about not being honest with her family and with herself. As you can imagine, truth and honesty have been a major part of my upbringing."

"So don't you think you are being dishonest now?" BJ asked. "Is secrecy not a form of not admitting what is happening and thus creating an untruth?"

"It is," Daniel said, "But I will tell her after my exams. I try to convince myself that withholding the truth isn't actually telling lies."

BJ laughed. "That's my boy!" he said and hugged his son. "Next time we meet you will have completed your exams, and then you'll have to decide where your qualifications are going to take you. Have you thought about that yet?"

"I certainly have, but I haven't come to a decision. I have discussed it with Professor Lingard and he put a few ideas to me. I can worry about that later once I know my results."

~ * ~

The week leading up to the degree ceremony was manic. Young men were buying staid grey and navy-blue suits as an alternative to wearing the psychedelic colours that were gracing the fashion stores in all their glory.

On the day of the ceremony, Lenny dared to wear lime green luminous socks with his navy-blue suit. "It's a token of respect to the times we are living in," he said. "These times are moulding our future. Free love and hippies are making a statement. We don't all have to adhere to that statement, but we can make our own. I'm planning to show the world what architectural progress we can make with our young and modern views."

"Good for you, Lenny. We can all face the world with enthusiasm and hopefully make our mark," Alison said. "We must all keep in touch and maintain this group as a significant part of the time we were in Birmingham together."

There were cries of agreement around as they went to line up with their respective faculties, all in caps and gowns, resplendent in fur trimmed, satin lined hoods in the representative colours of each department.

Daniel had gained a first-class honours degree in social sciences and politics. He hugged Alison before they went to join their lines. "We will keep in touch, won't we, Ali? I don't think my life will be complete without you."

"Dan!" she exclaimed. "Why has it taken so long to tell me that? I have wanted to let you know how I feel for yonks!"

Daniel shrugged. "I couldn't allow you to distract me, I guess," he said with an engaging smile.

Alison gave him a peck on the cheek. "Later," she said and winked at him as she left.

~ * ~

Emma had flown in a couple of days before the ceremony and stayed at The Midland Hotel. After the ceremony, she and Daniel intended to spend a few days travelling around England to visit the places she had always wanted to see but had never previously had the opportunity. She felt so proud as she walked through the heavy oak doors of the domed building with its impressive portico. Daniel had left her invitation at the hotel. She hadn't seen him, so she was extremely excited as she made her way to her seat, row D, seat number ten. She slid past the parents who were already in their allotted seats and, as she made herself comfortable, she checked to be sure her fashionable, pale blue linen suit was straight and not revealing too much leg. The seat to her right was vacant and she was grateful that she had somewhere to place her handbag instead of putting it on the floor.

Just before proceedings were due to start, the students lined up down the side of the hall and she tried to spot Daniel before he went up onto the stage. She looked to the left and then to the right...somebody was inching his way along the row to the vacant seat next to her. She wanted to run; she wanted to hide; she wanted the ground to swallow her whole. Panic set in and she found herself rooted to the spot.

"Hi, Emma," he whispered. "How are you?"

The ceremony proceeded and Emma sat in silence. She stared straight ahead, trying to focus on the master of ceremonies. Her mind was in turmoil. *I don't believe this. How can he possibly know that*

Daniel receives his degree today? I think I'm going to pass out. I can't breathe. I'm having a panic attack. Deep breaths, Emma, take deep breaths. Obeying her own instructions, she endeavoured to breathe easily without allowing her neighbour to notice the panic that was overwhelming her. *Why is he here? Don't cry,* she silently told herself. *Don't you dare cry as you did when you last saw him.* Suddenly, her thoughts were angry and self-justifying. *But why shouldn't I let him see the devastation he caused? I still feel the hurt in my heart. Why did he do that to me when our love was so strong? Did he use me for his own gratification?* She checked her thoughts again. *No! Not BJ. He loved me; I know he did. But he sent me away, didn't he?*

BJ stared straight ahead, too, not daring to look into the eyes of the woman he had loved and lost, the woman who had borne his child. *How she must hate me. My conscience has been my punishment for the past twenty years or more. How can I expect her to see me as the person I am now? She accepted me when I felt most vulnerable; she loved me, I know she did. I felt it in all its glory...the love, the passion, the sincerity in her feelings, the acceptance.* Breathing in deeply and letting the air flow slowly from his lungs, he chastised himself silently. *Shame on you, BJ Johnson. You don't deserve her. You didn't then and you don't now...but I still love her with all my heart and soul.*

Still concentrating on what was going on in front of her and with her initial feelings of panic subsiding, Emma's thoughts became more rational. *I walked away and left the country. I ran away because I felt unable to survive amongst those who couldn't, or wouldn't, accept how I felt about my man. Was I young and irresponsible? No, I don't think so.* She dared to sneak a quick peek at BJ whom, she observed, was sitting upright, tense and looking straight ahead as she had been just a few moments ago. Her heart skipped a beat, but she quickly became aware that Daniel was on the stage and about to receive his degree from the vice-chancellor of the university. She roused herself, stood and applauded as loudly she could.

BJ touched her arm as she returned to her seat. "Congratulations, Emma." He smiled endearingly. "You have done well." He wanted to say, *my darling Emma, I love you as I loved you twenty years ago and I'll love you for evermore if you will let me.*

Emma stiffened at his touch, but managed to say, "What are you doing here?"

BJ shrugged and studied his shoes.

Emma smiled at him. *Still the same endearing BJ,* she thought. *In spite of myself, I love him. I can't help it.*

They didn't notice when the rest of the parents on their row had all left their seats and they were the only two remaining. "Are you going to tell me what is happening?" she asked.

BJ shrugged, but looked up this time and took her hand. "I came to witness our son be presented with his degree. Same as you, I think."

She had not experienced that feeling deep within her soul for twenty-two years. "I feel like I used to feel on Christmas morning as a child," she said quietly. "Oh BJ, what have we done?"

"What we have done can be left in the past if you prefer," he said. "In my book, history does not repeat itself."

"Which book would that be, BJ? *The Devil's Hand* or *Belonging?*" she asked with an undeniable twinkle in her eye.

"You read them?" he asked as he took her in his arms and held her close. "The story starts now if you will allow it," he whispered, and feeling a tap on his shoulder, he turned to find Daniel and Alison hand in hand. "Did you engineer this?" he asked.

"It worked, didn't it?" Daniel said smiling, a sparkling, wonderful smile he had inherited from his father. "I knew it would! Alleluia! Now we can all belong together. End of story."

Meet Vera Berry Burrows

Vera Berry-Burrows is a UK-born former teacher of English Language and Literature, living in Queensland, Australia with former journalist husband, Alan. She has a son and two grandsons living in the UK. She has been writing for a number of years and has had numerous non-fiction articles published in the UK and in Australia. She was educated at Farnworth Grammar School in Lancashire, trained as a teacher at St Katharine's College, Liverpool and gained a Bachelor of Arts degree with the Open University, UK.

Since she took early retirement in 1994 having been in the teaching profession for thirty-one years, writing has become her compulsive hobby. *Skin Deep* is her eighth published novel.

Other Works From The Pen Of
Vera Berry Burrows

Tomorrow Never Comes - Relationships seriously affect the lives of a controlling mother, Nell Winston, and her rebellious son, Joel until the elusive tomorrows make all the earth-shattering yesterdays worthwhile.

Regarding Kimberley - Kimberley Mason unwittingly unearths a thirty-year-old dark secret kept by her parents when she forms links with a theatrical agency in Sydney, Australia.

Connections – Connections for better or worse, made by Jane O'Connell after divorce, completely disrupt her life, both shattering and illuminating her existence with unexpected consequences.

Family Matters - In war-torn Britain, John Hawthorne and three daughters, Meg, Patty and Abigail, rally forth on the battlefield of their own shattered lives.

My Name is Aphrodite - Rodi Bartlett's worldwide search for her father is relentless, because she knows that somebody somewhere made her from love.

Dare to Dream - Leaving an orphanage upbringing behind, two teenage girls need to learn how to survive in a world thus far alien to them.

Payback - Julietta's holiday becomes a nightmare when she is swept up in the frenzy of other people's abhorrent need for revenge.